CRUEL
CITY

GLOBAL AFRICAN VOICES
Dominic Thomas, EDITOR

CRUEL CITY

A Novel

Mongo Beti

Translated by Pim Higginson

INDIANA UNIVERSITY PRESS
BLOOMINGTON AND INDIANAPOLIS

This book is a publication of

Indiana University Press
601 North Morton Street
Bloomington, Indiana 47404-3797 USA

iupress.indiana.edu

Telephone orders   800-842-6796
Fax orders   812-855-7931

Originally published as *Ville Cruelle*.
© 1971 Présence Africaine
English translation © 2013 by Indiana University Press

Library of Congress Cataloging-in-Publication Data

Beti, Mongo, 1932–2001.
  [Ville cruelle. English]
  Cruel city : a novel / Mongo Beti ; translated by Pim Higginson.
    p. cm.
  Previous French edition: Nouvelle edition. Paris : "Présence africaine," 1971.
  ISBN 978-0-253-00823-7 (pb : alk. paper) — ISBN 978-0-253-00830-5 (eb)
1. Cities and towns—Fiction. 2. Cameroon—Fiction. I. Higginson, Pim. II. Title.
  PQ3989.2.B45V513 2013
  843'.914—dc23
  2012038561

1 2 3 4 5   17 16 15 14 13

CONTENTS

INTRODUCTION

COLLECTED HERE ARE TWO of the most important works of Francophone African literature, finally available in English: the critical essay "Romancing Africa" ("Afrique noire, littérature rose," 1955), and the novel *Cruel City* (*Ville cruelle*, 1954), both by the Cameroonian man of letters Alexandre Biyidi Awala, whom the world would come to know as Mongo Beti (1932–2001). Beti was born in the Northern Cameroonian town of Akométan near Mbalmayo, a city whose river and old reinforced concrete bridge can easily be imagined as models for Tanga. Indeed, numerous biographical details match up well with the novel, such as the early death of Beti's father and the discussions the author had with his mother about religion and politics. The big difference of course lies in the character's relative illiteracy. Over the course of his nearly fifty-year career, Beti would receive broad acclaim as one of the greatest literary tellers of political and existential truths; he spent decades in exile for his criticism of Cameroon's post-independence regimes, and his writing would, on occasion, even be censored in France. Both on their own and taken as the beginning of this substantial literary production, "Romancing Africa" and *Cruel City* represent a pivotal moment for the continent: the first drafts of a Francophone African literary canon.

"Romancing Africa" was published in the celebrated Paris-based journal *Présence Africaine*.[1] The young author's essay is a single-minded manifesto: a programmatic and radical break with the past; a bold challenge to colonialism and its various avatars; and a call to literary arms. Beti's first anti-establishment attack forcefully announces—demands, in fact—a path forward, toward a postcolonial African literary production. Along with its sheer brashness and daring, this youthful text also enumerates the challenges facing the sub-Saharan African novelist working in French. In summarizing these challenges, "Romancing Africa" first posits the total absence of quality literature in or on Africa, by which it means books that are actually read. By the essay's own account, this initial criterion immediately creates a series of problems. First, given the historical, economic, and cultural effects of colonialism, there is no African readership; only the French will consume such works. This French (bourgeois) readership thus single-handedly determines literary success; France controls the means of publication, distribution, and by extension, the terms of consumption.

According to Beti, the French reader in turn expects two things: that writing on Africa(ns) stress the folkloric; and that the colonial enterprise be celebrated, or at the very least not criticized. This latter expectation comes into immediate conflict with Beti's second determining criterion for a quality literary work, besides its popularity: that it objectively—that is to say critically—represent the effects of colonialism. Intervening literary history has thereby revealed Beti's two conditions for a quality African novel in French to be mutually exclusive. Indeed, any novelist wishing for success on the French literary scene will, according to Beti, avoid like the plague the truth of African modernity (its cities, its multiple engagements with global capital, its repressive administration, etc.); this author will necessarily dodge the complex and violent legacies of colonialism. Such a book, according to Beti, while popular, won't be a quality work of fiction because it won't be realistic, won't be honest about its subject matter. Significantly, this tension that Beti raised so succinctly almost sixty years ago remains in various forms at the heart of most African writing today, and certainly informs and shapes critical debates.

Of course, having established the essay's argument, how does "Romancing Africa" explain the author's own fiction? Or in other words, does Beti's text reach the author's own standards of excellence? If we hold him strictly to the very first rule, namely that the work should sell, the answer would have to be no. Despite its importance to the Francophone African canon, *Cruel City* has been through only three small printings in French. Regarding the second criterion, does *Cruel City* escape the fundamentally testimonial—what Beti calls the picturesque—expectations of a French readership? This is far more difficult to assess; rather, this question highlights Beti's ambivalence about where his character—indeed the African novel as whole—should go. "Romancing Africa" objects most strenuously to the representation of Africa as folkloric atemporal space; in this sense, to a Hegelian "timeless Dark Continent" Beti's novel opposes the historical present of a land coming to grips with its modernity, that is, with the colonial experience itself. What confuses matters is that the central protagonist, Banda, ultimately never makes the transition to the city; he remains caught in the maternal space of tradition that Odilia clearly represents. At the end of the novel, Banda knows he must listen to the one voice he trusts, namely his own, but can't quite yet bring himself to make the move . . .

While the relationship between the two texts is subject to interpretation, what we *can* infer from "Romancing Africa" is that *Cruel City* is experimental; the novel formulates its own conditions of possibility as it unfolds. As Banda makes his way from the countryside of Bamila to the city, Tanga, we witness the Francophone African novel transitioning to a new form. Not surprisingly, catching this movement challenges the process of translation, since questions concerning language lie at the heart of any manner of narrative exploration, and *Cruel City* is of course no exception. Because it is a series of experiments, the novel can appear—

or is—flawed: it drifts through phases of sentimentalism and is repetitive in parts. As I mentioned above, perhaps the story's most significant flaw is the absence of a convincing resolution. In sum, as its critics have often pointed out, this is not a mature work of fiction. At the same time, any heavy-handedness is the trace of the Promethean task the narrative performs; these faults are the immediate effect of the canon formation in which the novel is involved.

The novel's flaws resulting from its grand ambitions can be baffling for the translator; there are times when certain turns of phrase had to be modified, "corrected," or otherwise rendered more readable. At times I made such translational editing changes, but only with extreme caution and in highly selective cases since, taken as a whole, these shortcomings—if indeed they are such—are also precisely among the text's most interesting features. Beti's novel is a laboratory where modern Francophone African fiction is being deliberately wrought, almost out of thin air. The twist and turns of plot, the rhythm of the prose, all of which I have tried to reproduce in the English, constitute a series of trials (and errors) that explore the issues raised in "Romancing Africa." Ultimately, whether or not Beti succeeds is almost irrelevant: the novel is its own justification. In sum, "Romancing Africa" and *Cruel City* represent the theoretical and practical inauguration of an absolutely new kind of Francophone writing.

PIM HIGGINSON

NOTES

1. The journal, launched in 1947 by Alioune Diop, had heavy support from a number of famous French and African diasporic intellectuals, such as Frantz Fanon, Aimé Césaire, Richard Wright, Michel Leiris, and Jean-Paul Sartre, whose names would also appear prominently in its pages. It should be noted that Beti subsequently became disenchanted with what he saw as its over-coziness with French interests on the African continent.

ROMANCING AFRICA

Setting aside books written by explorers and missionaries, books where the thinking motivating their authors is so outdated that they are useless,[1] there is to my knowledge, not one quality literary work inspired by Black Africa and written in French. When I say a quality work, what I mean is something received, known, seen as such, by the public at large—because from the perspective of effectiveness, what might be the point of a masterpiece published in 1955 that will only be read and appreciated in the year 2000? It goes without saying that, for the purposes of my presentation, it wouldn't matter if the writer of such a work were Black or White. So, digressions aside, there is a complete absence of quality literary works in French inspired by Black Africa. Given the extensive research I have done, one would be hard pressed to contradict me on this last observation.

During the interwar years, it would have been easy to explain this dearth by the general lack of interest that Europe, and especially France, then had in Africa, and by Africans' inability to write in French due to a lack of training; in 1955, however, now that Africa is increasingly on Europe's mind and an ever greater number of Africans not only can but want to write, this absence of quality works is harder to fathom. Or so it might appear.

Look more closely and everything makes sense. To begin with, what kind of writer is interested in Black Africa?

You have the journalists, who are always stalking a new topic, and who, when they have located it, treat it for its novelty effect. The news stories written on Africa since the last war are particularly objectionable. It is difficult for journalists to write masterpieces on Africa.

You also have the intellectuals looking for a solution to the world of the future; they generally write semi-political, semi-philosophical, semi-literary narratives. This generates such works as "Naked People," by M[ax].-P[ol]. Fouchet, or again: "France and the Blacks," by Jean Guéhenno, to whom I will return shortly. Let me say up front that nobody is waiting for a masterpiece from this category of writer.

Then there are the industrialists, the politicians, the economists, and similar specialists. It would be best not to speak of them.

There are also the poets, some of whom are excellent: A[imé]. Césaire, D[avid]. Diop, Paul Nige, J[acques]. Roumain, etc. They are found most commonly among men of color, that is to say the colonized. These are generally highly aware, honest intellectuals, hence completely incapable of any sort of compromise with the colonial order; the result of this situation is that their voice isn't heard. Thus, in keeping with our idea of the masterpiece, I cannot accept what they are producing as quality works; as already noted, one cannot designate as a masterpiece, in terms of its present effectiveness, a work that nobody reads or knows about. I can only hope that the future will rehabilitate these *poètes maudits* [cursed poets]; but that's another story.

In fact, the category of writers from whom we expect the most are the novelists. I should note right off the interest generated by the publication of an African novel—assuming, of course, that the press is willing to talk about it. It is therefore specifically the case of African fiction that I will do my best to elucidate.

It so happens that, since the end of the last war, the novelists inspired by Black Africa are as often Whites as Blacks. This particular observation will turn out to be completely unimportant, as we will see shortly.

Instead, let's go straight to the heart of the problem and ask the essential questions.

First of all, what will be the overriding tone of the African novel, realistic or non-realistic? This will depend primarily on the temperament of each author, on his concern for the public's attitude. If the writer has no backbone, he will do what the public is asking for. If he has a backbone, he'll write according to his own taste and his own ideas. Figuring out what the French public wants from an African author is another question, one I will deal with a little later.

Next, what will be the central quality of this novel? It will depend primarily on its tone. Given modern conceptions of the beautiful in literature, at least what is essential in these considerations, if a work is realistic, it has an excellent likelihood of being good; otherwise, even assuming it has formal qualities, there is a high risk that it will lack resonance, depth, and most of all what great literature most pressingly needs: the human—from which we can surmise that it is far less likely to be good than a realistic work, if indeed there is any such likelihood at all.

As already mentioned, what will distinguish the African novelists is less their ethnic origin than their distinctive temperaments, their personalities. Indeed, it would seem, in theory at least, that only White writers would explore the folkloric side of Black Africa, whereas Black writers, more aware of their native continent's serious problems, would use folklore only as a way of underscoring Africa's deeper reality; but upon a close examination of the small number of authors writing on Africa, it becomes apparent that the folklorists can be found equally in both groups.

Among the Whites: *Knives At Play, Stick to Your Own Kind,* etc. . . .

Among the Blacks: *Black Child, The Gaze of the King, Karim,*[2] *Batouala,* etc. . . .

When I say "etc. . . ." that's actually just a figure of speech, for, though I was only going to cite those African authors specializing in folklore, I suddenly realize that I have named all the African authors to whom the French public and its critics have deigned pay attention in the last ten years.

Could it be that the French public asks for folklore, nothing but folklore, from the African author?

Besides, when I speak of the French public, of whom am I thinking exactly? Certainly not of the Africans, whose consumption of this foodstuff called literature is statistically negligible, at least for now, and this for reasons too complicated to explain in a journal article. I'll simply say that this illustrates the infamous drama of the uprooting of the African elite: African writers can't even write for a Black audience!

What remains is the Europeans' audience. Indeed, one has to admit that the African novelist, whether White or Black, writes primarily for the French reader of the Métropole, which explains an awful lot. But before going there, it's important to define the attitude of this public with respect to the African author.

The French-person-who-reads-novels—that is, in truth, the bourgeois, whether *petit* or *grand*—is not only a citizen but the pillar of a country that was, not long ago, a great nation, a nation that aspires to remain great, that hopes to regain that status, and a nation whose pride has been wounded daily since the war, something that happens to once-great nations. One doesn't need to be an expert on international affairs to realize that the properly European factors determining France's prestige are more irrevocably eroded each day.

Nevertheless, if this country refuses to cede its past greatness, what desperate measures will it employ, not only to achieve its hallowed rank among nations but to remain there? Why, the colonies, by God! The Empire! The French Union! Call it what you will. Never has the French bourgeoisie gambled so heavily on the colonies as at the present time.

But the colonies themselves—because of those little jokers the writers, the press, the educational system; because of those who, in certain spheres, are called the specialists of subversion—the colonies themselves, as I said, have learned and repeat to themselves [Pierre Victurnien] Vergniaud's famous call: "The great are only great because we are on our knees. Let us rise."[3] And the desire for autonomy and even separation in the French Empire only increases. Something previously unheard of has happened: one of the most prized countries in the Empire has waged a sustained war against the Métropole. That's not the end of it: another gem, the entire Maghreb, is facing a critical situation; and the truth is that nobody has a clue as to what is going to happen to this piece of the French Empire. Are we going to lose everything? Ask the colonizers and the French bourgeois, more worried than ever. "No, by God! Don't we still have Black Africa?"

For the colonizer and the French bourgeois, what is Africa? "An inexhaustible reserve of men and primary resources." (Here I am citing A[lfred]. Coste-Floret, Minister of the Colonies in one of the numerous governments of the first legislature of the Fourth Republic). We know the slogans: "Black Africa, our last chance!," "Black Africa, the card we should be playing!," "Eurafrica . . . ," etc. . . . The French bourgeois therefore thinks of Africa as his last remaining hunting grounds: a territory to be guarded jealously against the desires of so-called "revolutionary imperialisms." It goes without saying that behind all of the bourgeois press's well phrased liberal, generous, fraternal, and republican formulas there lies the same secular, intangible reality that is eternal cupidity: exploit man where and when you can without risk.

Yes, I said without risk! One can venture that these ladies and gents would not appreciate a realistic African literature, for what greater risk could there be that their operations should be denounced, dismantled, exposed in the popular press? They will therefore do everything to nip any realistic African literature in the bud. For the reality of Black Africa, its only true reality is before all else colonization and its crimes.[4]

Again, for those who aren't metaphysicians, the first reality of Black Africa, its only true reality, is colonization and what comes after it. Colonization, which today saturates every last inch of the African body and poisons its blood, suppresses every challenge. It follows that writing on Black Africa means being for or against colonialism. It's impossible to escape this equation. Even if one wanted to, one could not. Friend or enemy is the question at hand. Anybody who wants to escape this bind is forced to cheat.

It turns out that the bourgeois and the colonizers ask their scribes to cheat, to write in the name of their glory, to sing their praises. What happens then? If the scribe is a White man, he won't have the least compunction about writing the reactionary and racist books to which bookstores have habituated us: "Stick to your own kind [*Va-t-en avec les tiens*]," "Knives were drawn [*Les couteaux sont de la fête*]," etc.

If the scribe is Black, the operation becomes a little more difficult, since this Black person has to take into account the world from which he comes, his friends, his family. Besides, there resides in a Black person a kind of demureness; he's always loath to take a path that leads to prostitution; it's only once he has finally set out on that path that everything goes smoothly. Besides, one never knows; one day there could be a little revolution in his native country. And if he were there, even accidentally, might some not hold against him the fact that he had collaborated with the colonial enterprise?

The Black scribe will therefore pretend to not take sides. He will take refuge among the sorcerers, his grandfather's snakes, initiations at nightfall, fish-women, and the whole gamut of the two-bit picturesque. He will ignore all that might get him in trouble and particularly colonial reality. That's why, paradoxically, he will make himself even less realistic than the White scribe whose own position is without the least ambiguity. It turns out, however, that in the realm of the non-realistic, the Black scribe is better placed than the White scribe, because the ignorant bourgeois is more likely to pay attention to him. You see, when the Black scribe claims to have been initiated by moonlight, to have belonged to the brotherhood of lions, to have petted a sacred crocodile, etc., the bourgeois can receive these claims only with enthusiasm. "Now that's a guy who clearly knows what he's talking about! . . ." And that's the last word! All of this serves to further entrap the Black scribe in the quicksand of the folkloric, a mess from which it is difficult to extricate oneself. Under these circumstances the White scribe finds himself relegated to a secondary status.

If we refer to contemporary American literature, we discover what happens to a conformist writer, a friend of the high functionaries of those in power, who aspires to large print-runs. Ever since F. D. Roosevelt left power, Steinbeck has more or less stopped writing, Faulkner paraphrases the Bible (it's true that he's a special case), Hemingway has been content to develop a predictable myth in a little book received as his masterpiece, while a newcomer like Truman Capote, more logical than those who came before him, has deliberately chosen to go in the direction of the fantastic. In the same way, it would seem likely that an African writer, if he insists on dedicating his books to the great colonizers, will end up in the realm of the fantastic, assuming that's not where he starts.

Therefore, we are not in a time that is suited to an authentic African literature. This is because either the author writes realistically, in which case not only is he unlikely to be published, but even if he were, critics would ignore him, as would the public. Or he is a conformist, in which case he risks giving in to easy folklore and even to the fantastic, which will impel him to write mostly nonsense. As I have already said, I believe that in this particular case, race is of little importance—what counts is the temperament of the writer.

Still, another question needs to be asked: given the literary journals that exist in France, are there not two distinct and even opposed reading publics? More simply, aren't there on the one hand the readers of *Lettres françaises*, and on the other those of *Le Figaro littéraire*? Shouldn't the readers of *Lettres françaises* enthusiastically welcome a realistic African literature?[5]

It would appear that way, but only at first glance. On closer examination, things are far more complicated. In 1955, the world is divided into two powerful blocks, set against each in such severe antagonism that there is no room for those who refuse to take sides. Here, the dilemma that says: "He who is not with you works against you: friend or enemy, useful or harmful" is truer than ever. This century is constructed such that sectarian thinking has unapologetically taken over; people prefer their worst enemy to those among their friends who don't exactly replicate themselves.

Therefore, if, in the Metropolitan context an African writer is engaged neither totally on the Left nor totally on the Right, then he better keep quiet. Of course, it can happen that here or there, an individual succeeds in breaking down all the traditional barriers, in imposing himself against all odds, but it will nevertheless be the exception. So the France of 1955 suggests that the African author just keep quiet. Unless he should decide, not without a certain heroism, to write for that distant time when education will have sufficiently developed the taste for reading among his people, Africans. It seems that before then, it is impossible to speak of an authentic African literature. It also appears, to the extent that such things can be predicted, that such future literature will necessarily be not only African but even national: by which we mean that the African writer will speak to his co-citizens in the language they are looking for; he will speak to them about aspirations that they all have in common. Perhaps this literature, before it can aspire to a human and international level, will first have to be regionalist. And that will only be Europe's, and particularly France's, fault, since France has always been so self-involved that it refuses to see beyond the end of its own nose.

Having made the rounds of African literature in 1955, I wish to present to the readers of this journal two books, one written by a White man and the other by a Black man.

"France and the Blacks" by Jean Guéhenno[6]

This is a tiny little book of 140 pages that appeared in 1954. No pretension. Jean Guéhenno is an intellectual whose responsibilities as an educational inspector have brought him into contact with Black Africa. Mr. Guéhenno is not a journalist: thus his book is not a newspaper article (though it should be noted that his impressions all appeared in serial form in *Le Figaro littéraire*). Nor is it really an essay. So what is it? This book doesn't want to belong to any of the traditional categories, and that isn't a fault; rather the contrary, it is something commendable. To summarize, he reveals a French intellectual's impressions of Black Africa: the destiny, present and future, suggested to someone with the sort of generous heart occasionally found in our times. In introducing his book, Mr. Guéhenno says in most heartwarming fashion: "One hears a great deal said about the 'French Union.' It is a legal, economic, and political fact. One should be willing to admit that it is not yet a human fact since it is not yet in the hearts of men, whether Black or White. I only hope that these notes, as paltry as they may be, help in giving this 'French Union' life."

The author has been through and around a good portion of French West Africa. He has visited many places: Dakar, Bamako, Bobo-Dioulasso, Ouagadougou, Niamey, Lomé, Abidjan. He has observed, he has meditated, and he now gives us the fruits of these meditations on his observations. And, it should be said that it is a very good read. But as I was saying earlier, one should have no illusions about this kind of work, and Guéhenno himself recognizes this fact: "I am under no illusion," he says on page 56, "about what is artificial in this kind of a voyage. Having completed my day's work, today in two hours I was able to see, for my amusement, the market, the governmental palace, the river and its port . . . the biggest café where the Whites get married and unmarried and so on and so forth. We fly through the air, we run along the trails. We are now on our ten thousandth kilometer . . . I don't know what good I will have done for humanity, but I fear that upon my return, though innocent, I will have the Green Cross at my heels."

It is true that Guéhenno spares neither natives nor Europeans. He's even honest enough to admit that: "In Dakar one feels no human warmth. Blacks and Whites are brought together there despite themselves, incapable of looking at each other. I can barely breathe. As soon as I am free, I escape . . ." And later: "One becomes obsessed here with the problem of racial confrontation. Perhaps there is no solution to it . . ." But in the final analysis? The colonizer and the bourgeois close the book with a conscience even clearer than before. I, for my part, close this book with rage because I feel I have been duped. The title! . . . And without so much as blinking an eye, the gangsters of colonialism continue their infernal work, assured that if ever their lives or possessions were at risk, the Foreign Legion would parachute from the sky like manna from heaven—and that's the truth. At no time has the crux of the problem been touched upon.

Let's not ask for too much from this man of good will and let us forgive him because he wasn't an economist, a politician, a revolutionary, or a specialist in one thing or another; because he was an amateur simply talking "in abondantia cordis"; and especially because he was writing for *Le Figaro littéraire*. And yet let's reread his book, recognizing all the while the gift he has deigned bestow upon us, we Africans whose ingratitude is now proverbial in colonial circles! . . .

L'Enfant noir

This Guinean irresistibly seduces us. His exuberance is overflowing with poetry, a poetry that rises from a spring—this despite, it should be recognized, a few clichés and here and there, a questionable choice of words. It is as if he could barely sit still, carried away again and again by the breathless rhythm of violently colored village and pastoral scenes. He has chosen to move in a world where different modalities confuse themselves at will, for our reading pleasure. If he shows a certain tendency toward garish romanticism and a certain verbosity, it is that he is paying the ransom for an unexpected kinship with . . . Tibulus! I have forgotten to mention his sensibility, a sensibility that is perhaps clumsily exploited, but that is perhaps his greatest asset. Camara Laye is an authentic poet.

Nevertheless, there are people who will be disappointed by his book. And first and foremost, us, of course; we young Africans who have lived the same adventure as Laye, give or take a few details; we, for whom the promising title and the family name of the author made us believe for a second that this would be the great book about our childhood—that we still await! (Despite Camara Laye and his brilliant qualities). Additionally, for those who have read Richard Wright's pathos-ridden *Black Boy*, there will be an inevitable comparison between the two books, and the monstrous absence of vision and depth of the Guinean's book will be evident. Particularly for those who, in the final analysis, believe that the century demands of the writer—believe that it is a categorical imperative—that he refuse gratuitous art, that he reject the idea of art for art's sake.

To be honest, what is at stake here is much less the book itself than the mentality of which it is the nauseating product. Wright—since the title of Laye's book also represented a kind of challenge—refuses to make the least concession to the public, presents the problems at hand in all of their crude reality, avoids clichés, anything superfluous, anything naïve. Laye, for his part, is perfectly content to use the most harmless and easiest—which is to say the most lucrative—kind of folklore; he erects the cliché into an artistic approach. Despite appearances, he insists on showing us a stereotyped image—and therefore a false one—of Africa and of Africans: an idyllic universe, the optimism of overgrown children, stupidly interminable festivities, circus-act initiations, circumcisions, excisions, superstitions, Uncle Mamadou, images whose recklessness is only equaled by their unreality. It is true that Laye touches on subjects that might have given his story value; unfortunately, he only does so from a vantage point that is borrowed from some kind of "Tales from the Bush and Forest" or "Mamadou and Binéta Have Grown Up." One can only pity him when he speaks of the totem, of spells, of genies. In sum, there is nothing in this book that a European petit bourgeois won't have heard of on the radio, in some article he might run into anywhere, or any tired old program playing on "France Soir."

On the other hand, Laye closes his eyes to the most crucial realities, precisely those that have always been hidden from the public here. Is this Guinean, my fellow African, who is, or so he suggests, a lively and attentive boy, saying that he never saw anything but a peaceful, beautiful, and maternal Africa? Is it remotely possible that he didn't once witness the slightest atrocity on the part of the colonial administration?

Finally, *Black Boy* is not a testimonial—my God! When I think of the conclusions to which some of the people I know will come . . . —despite the ambitious (I mean tantalizing!) title.

Also, an African good sense that condemns a lack of intellectual integrity demands that Camara Laye redeem himself. This should be an easy task for someone so obviously talented. We await him at the next turn, which is to say his next book.

A.B. [Mongo Beti]

Notes

1. Here I'm especially thinking of a Monsignor Augouard, then a simple priest, who declared to his mother in one of his numerous letters that, now that he was living among the Blacks, he was absolutely certain that they were the descendants of Ham—an ancestry that was apparently highly unfortunate under the pen of this particular prelate. And indeed, he recognizes in the next sentence that he has no proof to back up this assertion; nevertheless, he insists that these are the real descendants of Ham. Today, Europe no longer finds it necessary to justify its African adventure in so paltry a manner.

2. I have given myself permission to cite these titles written before the war, such as *Batouala*, and *Karim*. My thinking here is that even though these

books don't belong to the period or the field that I had given myself as an object of study, they might be of use to the reader curious about African literature.
   3. Translator's note: This quotation is in fact from Pierre Joseph Proudhon.
   4. I know that there will be no end of people to accuse me of a bias, of lacking in objectivity, of seeing only one facet of colonization, without even bothering to look at the other: its benefits. Indeed, European rhetoric, especially French rhetoric, demands that every reality have two sides: an ugly one and a beautiful one. Nevertheless, if we examined the war from this perspective, wouldn't we risk justifying it? That being said, it is true that Hitler's regime had already done this. In my opinion, the war and colonization are connected in that respect, as in many others: they cannot be judged according to the methods of argumentation taught in the last year of high school; colonization, like war, is entirely ugly or entirely beautiful; finding them both ugly and beautiful at the same time is but a vulgar self-justification.
   5. *Lettres françaises* is a literary and cultural journal heavily trending toward the Left. From 1953 to 1972, its chief editor was the communist Louis Aragon, and at the outset the paper was heavily funded by the French Communist Party. Conversely, *Le Figaro littéraire* trends heavily to the Right.
   6. Published by the Editions Gallimard.

CRUEL CITY

1

"I'M THE MOST MISERABLE GIRL of them all. Think about it, Banda. Women mock me relentlessly in their songs. The old folks pity me. When I walk by, the young can barely turn away; they can hardly keep from laughing. But I'm not holding any of this against you. I still need to know why you did this to me. Why didn't you want me? All I need is an explanation."

Fearing this discussion yet anticipating it, Banda cast a melancholy gaze on his girlfriend: he examined her face with a combination of annoyance and pity. He was visibly perplexed. His whole body, particularly his mouth, expressed the distaste of the generous spirit in the face of life's demands.

He turned his gaze away just as languidly as he had looked in her direction and buried his head in the filthy yellowing pillow as if it held the answer. He remained stretched out on the bed among the filthy sheets. His long lean body evoked those gigantic black snakes suffering from indigestion that one occasionally crosses in the fields.

In the nearby brush, a few straggling partridges continued to call each other from place to place. A clear, noisy, and turbulent morning forced its way in through the roof and the cracks in the door. Outside, roosters began to stir, crowed at the top of their lungs, and mumbled a few gallant phrases. Banda closed his eyes as if he wanted to ignore it all, wanted to forget.

In a tired, halting, yet undeterred voice, she resumed her interrogation.

"Tell me why you refuse to marry me. How could you prefer a kid who will never know how to cook? I, on the other hand . . . and besides, you'd never have to pay for a thing."

"You're annoying me," Banda blurted out suddenly. It was a cry of despair rather than anger. She sat at the very edge of the bed. Both unsettled and curious, she examined this overgrown boy, this man who suddenly appeared to her in a completely new light. Yes, men were all cruel and insensitive. A stifling and pregnant silence followed. Then Banda spoke.

"What exactly were you thinking? That I had to marry you because you feed me beef—and I wonder where you get it, though again, I'd rather not know . . . and because you let me between your sheets? So, am I to understand that this is a transaction? Why didn't you say so immediately?"

Just as quickly he was silent again, then he sighed. Perhaps he already regretted the outburst, that it went too far. Perhaps he was just relieved, realizing suddenly that he had just ended their relationship and that this was one less thing to worry about.

She broke the silence in a voice that remained hesitant but determined.

"I'm no longer asking you to marry me; simply tell me why you're abandoning me. How can you have forgotten the time we spent together, the things you said to me, that I was beautiful, that I was the only woman in the world with whom you were truly at ease? Did I do something that made me undesirable? Did . . . Tell me, I need to understand . . . "

Banda said nothing. After a short pause, he imprudently blurted out:

"My mother!"

"What about your mother?"

"Yes, my mother. She feared that you'd become sterile. Rumor had it that you slept with so many men . . . "

He avoided her gaze, which he could feel lashing his face.

"Banda," she whispered, softly pursing her lips, "you should be ashamed! Your mother said that and you just accepted it? Will you always be a child? Your mother will soon be dead; can't you see that?"

Deep down she was ecstatic. What the young man's confession also revealed was that the "kid" wouldn't be a significant obstacle. But Banda's piercing gaze put an end to any such hope.

"You see," he confided, as if half regretting it, "for me, my mother is . . . Oh! What good is it; you couldn't possibly understand. As you know, I barely remember my father."

Lying on his back, he stared obstinately at the smoke-blackened thatch of the roof. His sentences were interspersed with heavy pauses.

"I only had my mother," he continued.

"And the others?" she snapped.

"What others?"

"Other boys your age . . ."

"What about them?"

"Few of them got to know their fathers. They only had their mothers. That doesn't mean they worship them as if they'd invented the world. Am I right?"

Banda exhaled deeply. Was he going tell her everything? He was overwhelmed by weariness, as he was whenever he faced an impossible task.

"No, it's not the same thing," he said, looking at her pleadingly. "Listen carefully."

He had turned toward her; while he spoke, bracing himself on one elbow, he gesticulated wildly with his free hand, as if to give his explanation more plausibility. In the face of her dark and ardent stare, he soon realized that she would never understand. He therefore promptly rolled onto his back, stretching out full length, losing his gaze in the thatch. One would have thought that he was now speaking for himself, or at least an invisible audience.

"I love my mother. Aiiii! I love her in a way you couldn't possibly understand. Have you ever loved someone? When my father died, I was only a couple of years old. My mother took on the task of raising me; she gave this responsibility all her attention. She did absolutely everything for me, you hear? She stuffed me with food. Good food. She administered a colonic once a week. Every night she put me into an enormous kettle of warm water and scrubbed my entire body. Three times a week she sent me off to the catechist . . . I was better dressed than those kids my age who had fathers. We slept on bamboo cots on either side of a fire that my mother stoked continuously while she told me stories, or spoke of my father, or of her own childhood, or of the country where she was born, or of my grandmother who died shortly before I was born. On some nights we would hear an owl hoot or a chimpanzee howl; I would curl up in my bed and my mother, laughing all the while, would say, 'Don't be scared, son. He's not going to come get you while I'm here . . .' On other nights, the rain drummed on the roof while violent gusts of wind swept through the courtyard, shaking the trees outside the village; then my mother would say: 'My God! Listen to the mangoes fall. Aren't you going to be happy tomorrow? Am I right?' Oh, she punished me often and without mercy, all right. But the memory of those whippings makes her all the more precious.

"Everything she was became clear to me the first time I suffered. My mother had registered me at the city school. From then on I was away from her five days a week. That day, I cried in a way I'll never cry again." He leaned over and spat on the floor. "I finally got used to this new existence: but in the beginning it was very difficult; because of my mother's jealousy I wasn't used to being around other children. At school, I was stubborn, gloomy, timid, always close to tears. This always annoyed my playmates and led to frequent punishment . . .

"Every Saturday, my mother came to the city. On Sunday, she'd take me to mass, where I'd just yawn. She would leave at the end of the day, but not without a few tender words, that she loved me, that she constantly thought of me, and that she prayed God that nothing bad would happen. Nevertheless, without my knowing it, I was growing up, getting tougher. I was becoming a man. I had already begun to think less frequently about my mother. I had other worries. Her visits, her words, her piety, began to embarrass me. She was fully aware of the changes happening in me. But, precisely because of my age, her sense of propriety prevented her from criticizing me for certain things. How she must have suffered! I only figured this out much later.

"I had been laboring away for eight years in their school, planting, harvesting potatoes, never doing what one normally does at school. Finally, they decided that I was too old and they kicked me out, without a diploma of course.

"Because my mother had stopped visiting, I hadn't seen her in a while. Once I was reunited with her, I could barely recognize her. She was already ill with the strange sickness that continues to drain the life out of her. She had sacrificed too much in raising me. And I had given her so little thought! If she remained in this hostile country among my father's half-brothers, people who despised her because they knew she didn't have any respect for them, it was for me." Once more, he leaned over and spat on the floor. "To think that she could have returned to her native country where she had relatives. But no, my father wanted me to take up the family land in Bamila. She didn't have the right to leave, to deprive me of my own land. Frankly, I was wracked with remorse. Thinking back, I imagine her bent over in the baking sun, resolutely scratching the earth with a miniature hoe or going to the market loaded down with a basket of vegetables; all this for me, and I had forgotten her so quickly . . .

"I wanted to redeem myself. I started arguments with those I thought had made her life difficult since my father's death. I was strong . . . The result? Everyone in the village hates me now, and I'm glad. Nothing is greater than the love of a mother for her child. Perhaps I'm exaggerating; but my mother loved me too much for me to think otherwise."

He paused at length. His chest suddenly expanded more than usual and he let out a violent breath. Seated at the very edge of the bed she continued to observe him with the same curiosity tinged with reserve.

"It's true. My mother will soon be dead. When that happens I'll simply go to the city. It isn't that I want my mother to die. No, that's not what I want. Still, she'll be dead soon. And then I won't be able to continue living here; there won't be any reason for it. I'll leave the country, the village, and I'll go try my luck in town."

"What will you do in the city?"

"I'll try to work. But don't be misled; it goes without saying that I won't marry you. I won't disobey my mother even if she's dead. The dead walk among us. It's true that I haven't been a model son, but at least in that respect. . . ."

"And the kid? Does your mother like her?"

"Well, she came to the house, my mother took a look at her; all she said was, 'She's a beautiful woman.' That's it. She doesn't particularly like her."

She was panting a little, as if she'd run to catch up with Banda, who she sensed was irrevocably escaping her grasp. The same person she always thought of as a big baby was now crushing her. Their eyes locked. She commented without much conviction:

"Would you really pay that much for that miserable waif?"

His stare was almost severe, almost condescending as he answered her.

"The fact is that I like her . . . Don't you get it, my child? It's because of my mother. She wants me to wed before she dies. It will be her dying joy. I can't deny her that pleasure. And since this is the only woman that my mother hasn't explicitly rejected . . . "

Outside, the morning was already bright with sunshine and blue sky. Banda was suddenly ready to leave . . .

"Tomorrow," he announced, "I'm going to the city to sell my cocoa to the Greeks. I hope those sons of thieves will give me enough money for the business I have in mind. On the off chance that you needed something . . . "

Without really knowing how, she understood that it was finally over. She didn't express any particular need.

Now alone, she couldn't help but feel sorry for herself. That brat really wasn't the woman he needed.

WHAT HAS BECOME OF THE CITY of Tanga since the events described in this story? As if anything could really happen in so few years! Today, everything is racing ahead in Africa, yet what upheavals could the city have possibly experienced? One can only hope for some manner of change; it would simply be too painful to accept such downtrodden people unless the city were marching boldly toward a less ferocious destiny; unless it were feverishly crossing a night that will soon give way to the sharp brightness of day.

At that time, Tanga certainly looked like other cities in the country: corrugated iron, white walls, red gravel streets, lawns, and farther out, scattered about with no apparent order, little mud huts roofed with dull thatch, naked children in the mud, or on the grass of the courtyard, with housewives on the stoop. Yet, upon arriving in Tanga, the astonished visitor might say, though perhaps only to himself, "There's something different about this city!" Tanga didn't lack for distinction.

Imagine an immense clearing in what explorers, geographers, and journalists like to call the equatorial rainforest. Picture, in the middle of this clearing, a large hill bordered by smaller ones. Tanga, or what was in reality two Tangas, sat on the opposing flanks of this central rise. The commercial and administrative Tanga sat on one, while the other—the foreign—Tanga occupied the steep and narrow southern flank. This latter part of the city was cut off from the nearby forest by a deep dark river spanned by a reinforced concrete bridge. The river was one of Tanga's main attractions, a kind of permanent circus. One only had to look and wait. Soon, a houseboat would sweep into view upstream. It would slide softly through the water, one man standing in the bow and one in the stern. Each would lift a long, a very long pole: each in turn would plunge that pole down into the water until it hit bottom. Then they pushed off with all their might, thereby moving the vessel along.

Inside the boat, bulging bags were piled up against the bamboo railing; a woman squatting on the deck washed tattered clothes next to a smoking kitchen fire. The crowd amassed on the bridge never got tired of this spectacle; these huts mounted on lashed-together canoes had traveled hundreds of kilometers. The craft would come heavily to rest on the sand, one next to the other.

Sometimes it was enormous logs of wood that had been lashed together. These rafts likewise came from far away. These were steered by men, usually naked, who were superbly indifferent to the catcalls that drifted down from the bridge. They calmly maneuvered their craft up to the log station. Once they had arrived, one of the two cranes stationed on the wharf would clatter into action. Panting and grinding, rolling along its track, it moved toward the river. Then it stopped and leaned dangerously over the water; it finally came upright again with a log clenched in its teeth. Then it turned and was gone. It was a monstrous object. It would be hard to imagine anything uglier.

This machine made an elephant look handsome. The crane proceeded to pile the logs in a lot where one could hear the angry snap of axes smoothing off the tree trunks, rounding out their rough edges, reducing them to dimensions fit for the factory and for civilization. A miserable wheezy little train arrived from a nearby depot without a station and picked up the load of newly squared logs. It carried them off, bleached and numbered, lying on the train cars in well-behaved rows, heading God knows where.

On this side of the town, everything seemed to live for these logs, all the way to the sawmill in the distance, where one could make out gangly chimneys rhythmically spewing forth clouds of smoke into the sky. Here the log was king.

Climbing up the hill, one entered Tanga's commercial center. The "commercial district," as it was known, could have just as easily been called the Greek district. All the store signs sounded Greek: Caramvalis, Depotakis, Pallogakis, Mavromatis, Michalides, Staberides, Nikitopoulos—and so forth. Their shops were built at ground level with verandas where indigenous tailors set up shop with their apprentices. You could find absolutely everything in these stores. Behind the counter, Black clerks and their assistants warmly, indeed, too warmly, invited you in. Theirs was the place where you would find the best prices. Theirs was the place where you would find the highest quality merchandise.

You rarely saw the Greek boss, except during the cocoa season, that is, from December to February (for if down below wood was king, here cocoa reigned supreme). So eight o'clock was ringing and Mr. Pallogakis—hair slicked back, olive-skinned, fresh looking, soberly garbed in white, lean, a hooked and paternalistic nose—was already at his post in front of a steelyard, surrounded by his men, beaters who cried out, vociferated, stamped about frantically, and slapped their thighs. From afar, they sang the praises of their boss with a few colorful and evocative words. If you appeared disdainful, they came into the street, grabbed you by the collar, and said, "Put down your load right there, on the sidewalk, we'll put it back on your head if need be. Listen to us. Sixty francs a kilo . . . Think about it, brother. Where else will you find such a price?" And so it went. Mr. Pallogakis started the day with a rate that was higher than the official price: the news spread like wildfire. The peasants came running with their bags. And the more there were, the more came rushing in, the easier it became for Mr. Pallogakis to progressively and imperceptibly lower his price and commit various other forms of fraud.

The incessant traffic in Tanga gave it a distinct drama. For example, no day passed without someone being
crushed by an automobile or a spectacular crash between
two trucks. Indeed, there seemed to be too many trucks in
Tanga. Perhaps this was simply because they came from the
four corners of the earth: each factory had sent at least one
such vehicle to represent it. There were long bony ones that
looked like a prehistoric animal; others were gigantic and
full bodied and made enough noise to drive you mad; still
others were short and squat. They came from the North, the
South, the East, and the West, all at insane speeds. Without
slowing down, they barreled into the city, leaving a triumphant cloud of dust in their wake, or they splattered everyone and everything with red mud: the streets of Tanga
weren't paved at the time of this story.

This commercial district ended at the peak of the hill
with a block of administrative buildings that were too
white, too showy. They sparkled in the sun, the sight of
them for some unknown reason giving off an implacable
sense of desolation.

The other Tanga, the unspecialized part of the city, the
Tanga to which the administrative buildings turned their
backs—out of a lack of appreciation, no doubt—was the
Tanga that belonged to the natives; this Tanga—of huts—
fanned out over the northern flank of the hill. This particular area of the city was divided into innumerable little
neighborhoods, though these were actually just a series of
little dips in the landscape, each of which had an evocative name. You could see the same kinds of buildings that
you might encounter along the road through the forest except that here they were more decrepit, squatter; they were
constructed in a manner corresponding to the increased
difficulty of obtaining materials the closer you got to the
city.

Two Tangas . . . Two worlds . . . Two destinies!
These two Tangas held equal sway over the locals. During the day, the Tanga of the Southside, the commercial

district of money and wage labor, emptied the other Tanga of its human substance. The Black population filled up the Tanga where it worked. The streets then came alive with workers, peddlers, cooks, servants, dishwashers, prostitutes, functionaries, underlings, beaters, con artists, the lazy, and forced laborers. Each morning, the peasants of the local forest would join the existing mass of people, either because they just wanted to broaden their horizons, or because they needed to sell the product of their work; among the locals, a particular mentality had arisen that was so contagious that the men who periodically arrived from outside were contaminated as long as they remained in the city. Like those of the distant forest who retained their authenticity, the people of Tanga were apathetic, vain, too playful, and overly sensitive. But on top of that, there was something else in them now, a certain inclination toward venality, apprehension, alcoholism, and everything that reflects a disregard for human life—as is the case in any country where material interests are paramount. The city held the record for murders . . . and suicides! One killed or killed oneself over everything, over anything, sometimes even over a woman. It even happened that a Greek would be gunned down because of his penchant for fondling women, as long as they were pretty and had entered his store. One day, the husband would burst into the store with a rusty old hunting rifle or, for lack of anything better, a bush knife, and without further ado, would punch his ticket.

The locals' love of fighting and blood grew daily. When they had had enough of working each other over, they turned to the phenomenal number of merchants who lived there. They had quickly discovered that they could conduct this little game—of which nobody knew the tricks or rules—with impunity. One simply had to avoid confronting the French. But if the latter should happen, you knew what to expect. After all, isn't that the most important thing? Out of bravado, certain people accepted the risk. The police nabbed these folks immediately, and that was the last one ever heard of them—unless they were still talked about decades later. As for the civilian members of the colonial administration's hierarchy, they seemed to be paid to remain as invisible as possible.

The local population had therefore arrived from the four corners of the country. But they increasingly thought of themselves as inhabitants of Tanga rather than coming from the South, East, North, or West. One could observe them in the streets: they laughed, talked, and argued, all with exaggerated gestures that suggested that they were the masters of the universe. They ran, walked, bumped into each other, and fell off their bicycles, all with a certain spontaneity, all that remained of their lost innocence. They moved, danced, and sang under the nervous eye of the guardians of order whose rounds made the city look like it was in a permanent state of emergency.

At night, activity changed headquarters. North Tanga brought its people home and suddenly it became incredibly alive. Every night, it celebrated the return of these prodigal children. It seemed as if North Tanga needed to quench their thirst for something they might soon lose forever: joy, naked and real; happiness. But this they couldn't understand. They could no longer say where they came from except by naming their village or tribe. They didn't know where they were going or why. Indeed, they were surprised to find themselves part of such a crowd, and no less astonished at the strange sense of isolation produced by the surrounding tropical forest in which they felt themselves individually.

In North Tanga, one out of five huts served as a bar: watered down red wine, poorly stored palm wine, and corn meal beer—usually the best choice—flowed liberally. Those in the know could also find Africa gin, a famous local beverage with a very high alcohol content. The administration had officially made the pretense of outlawing its sale . . . and its distillation. An illegal network of distribution, purchase, sale, and transportation of this rare beverage had accordingly been set up. In any case, they couldn't actually prohibit its fabrication since they didn't bother to look at what was happening in the forest.

The dance houses also represented an irresistible attraction to inhabitants of both sexes and were violently lit, melodious, and, more often still, cacophonic, percussive, and full of a singular fauna. Dressed up in detachable cardboard collars, or stuffed into poorly tailored dresses and skirts, they wore clothes that were stiff, gaudy, borrowed, and fake. Luckily, they didn't cost much. The dancers also frequently gathered by twos, threes, or more, around a calabash of wine, beat an empty crate for lack of drums, while someone picked at a guitar or banjo, thereby improvising a party where fantasy was the rule despite the locale's barrenness.

It goes without saying that there was no public lighting in Tanga. The numerous local thugs took advantage of this to transform the streets into a place where scores could be settled. That is why the darkness constantly echoed with the sound of heavy steps, frenetic chases, and blows that popped like a Browning pistol. These episodes of brutality, by force of habit, had come to be of interest only to those they directly impacted; the rest of the population remained completely indifferent. Because good fiscal management and a sense of prudence dictated a total absence of policing in this part of town, to a stranger, these fights could last a disconcertingly long time.

So, how many souls called North Tanga home? Sixty, eighty, one hundred thousand, how could you tell? No census had ever been taken. Besides, the population was in a constant state of flux. Men left the forest for financial or sentimental reasons; or often out of a need for change. They stayed for a while, testing out the city. A few decided that it was unthinkable to dance in one hut while the neighboring house was mourning someone whose body remained unburied, and, disgusted, they simply returned to their village, where they spoke of the city with sadness, wondering what the world was coming to. Others, convinced it would just take time to get used to such odd customs, settled down for good. These men sent for their wives and children or, if they were young and single, brought their younger brother or sister along as a constant and living reminder of the village they might never see again, and then, little by little, as the years went by, they forgot it, instead focusing on problems of an entirely different nature. Some, deciding that they couldn't fulfill their ambitions in Tanga, moved on to another city.

All the same, this instability couldn't justify the absence of a census, since the administration was completely unaware of these movements. It was equally unaware of this semi-humanity's joys, its sufferings, or its aspirations, all things, which, no doubt, it would have found confusing. It had never tried to discern, to understand, or to account for any of this. When it did finally deign to pay any attention to these people, two categories appeared to be particularly sought after. First, those who, having made it past innumerable stumbling blocks, had somehow achieved a semblance of social ascendance: the treasury suddenly decided that for this group a little taxation might be appropriate. Second, those who, from close or afar, consciously or unconsciously, by deed or by word, threatened the order of things, a particular conception of the world deemed necessary for certain reasons, or for that matter a particular group's interests; in the case of this latter type, things were simple: they were given full room and board somewhere and all would be back to normal, for the greater glory of humanity.

Tanga, North Tanga that is, was a true child of Africa. It had barely been born when it found itself alone in the great wilderness. It grew and developed too rapidly. It moved and evolved at random, its inhabitants like children abandoned to their own devices. Like them, the city didn't question its own fate, even when confused. No one could say what the city would become, not the geographers, not the journalists, and even less the explorers.

3

ONE FEBRUARY MORNING IN 193 . . . , in a low hut on the outskirts of Moko, one of the neighborhoods of North Tanga, two young people, two children really, were getting ready to face the new day. They had faced many before, just as they hoped to face many more. They didn't look like each other, even though they were brother and sister. He was young, rather tall, and somewhat stocky. With his long arms, his long trunk, his slightly short legs, he was one of the more common physical types around these parts. What distinguished him was his ever so slightly reddish complexion. His hair revealed a similar tint that a stranger would have thought unexpected. Even so, up close, there was not doubt that he was a child of this land. His slightly too light and disconcertingly darting eyes finally revealed the truth of this mystery: he had albino blood.

She, for her part, gave an immediate and overwhelming impression of radiant beauty. She was well proportioned, strong-boned but supple, with a slightly prominent backside. Her ample chest stretched the poorly cut cotton dress that signaled "village girl." She had the smooth dark skin of a girl who bathes every day, slightly chubby cheeks, large sad eyes, and abundant hair woven into braids that fell toward her neck. The sum of her movements seemed a compendium of maternal promise.

After having donned his once-khaki mechanic's uniform that had become oily, dirty, and black, he came into the little common room and rested his elbows on the sill of the small opening that served as a window: he kept his back to his sister and seemingly paid her no attention. He whistled girls' songs as he watched the women going to market on the dusty roadway in compact and talkative clusters. From time to time he would call one out, always a pretty one, giving her the name of the color dress she was wearing: "Blue Poplin." When she turned toward him, he would say something with suggestive undertones; she would come back with the conventional retort and both would burst out laughing. Sometimes, he would stop joking and even cease whistling and then his gaze would become lost in the distance. But this would only last an instant before he would catch himself, knowing that his sister was watching.

A siren sounded in the distance. He turned around nonchalantly, walked toward the little wooden table to pick up his old hat, and noted that it had been set. His sister, now leaning against the wall, watched him from the corner of her eye, questioningly. He took the lead:

"Odilia, my sister!"

"Hmm," she grudgingly said.

Perhaps he was going to talk about some inane topic in order to hide his true feelings?

"Odilia," he started again, "how am I to understand this? It's been ages since we had any money and yet we eat. How do you do it, little sister?" He was laughing heartily.

"The surrounding villages are full of good people," she answered, deliberately avoiding the question.

"One has to believe that some divine providence is watching over the poor Black folks," he noted in lieu of a comment, as he ate. "Of course food isn't really a problem: you could always go back to the village to get it. Besides, I don't give a damn; I've gone weeks without chewing on a thing, just drinking water. You, on the other hand, have to eat and eat well . . ." He paused, perhaps because he ate fast in order not to be late and his mouth was too full, or perhaps because he was scared of saying too much. She looked at him suspiciously. That dream! Did he really look as if he were going to die today? She tried to picture his face frozen in a death mask—she couldn't do it. No, it wasn't possible, she told herself. There was nothing resembling a dead body in him! What silliness to believe in dreams. Still, though she could tell herself it was stupid, her mind drifted back to the idea anyway. She felt like crying until her heart broke, as she had last night in her dream . . .

"I'll soon find work with someone nicer than that T. . . . But I just can't leave him like that."

"And why not?" she begged, with tears in her eyes.

"No! Never!" he cried out banging his fists against the table. "If people start paying us only when and if they feel like it, how, I ask you, are we going to live? Oh, he'll pay! He'll have to show up. Oh, heck! Why talk about this here? . . ."

She leaned deliberately against the wall, facing her brother. One could make out a glow of defiance in her gaze.

"Beware, Koumé," she warned. "You've never been prudent. You think you'll always make do as you have in the past, isn't that right? I'm not so sure. Be careful! Your Mr. T. is friends with the police commissioner . . ."

"I know. But don't forget that I have my own friends."

He had gotten up. He put on the old hat that gave him an impersonal look, made him look just like millions of his compatriots.

"My little Odilia, know this: we have the numbers and we are in the right."

"Others before you have had those things. Don't you have eyes?"

He was kidding. He loved to tease his "kid sister," as he called her. He was smiling, relaxed.

One couldn't have guessed that he was working out various plans in his mind.

"Are you going to harm him?"

Caught unprepared, he turned around suddenly, his lips trembling, haggard, taken aback like a boxer who's just received a low blow. He hesitated to answer.

"No," he finally ventured, without much conviction. And as if his conscience bothered him, he added: "What are you worried about? Leave it be; this is boys' business. You'll find out . . ."

He stopped on the doorway, whistling, as if it were any other fine day. He turned to his sister one last time and said, "Goodbye, little sister. Don't worry. I know how to handle dust-ups with bastards like T. . . ."

And he disappeared.

This wasn't just idle talk. He really believed what he said.

4

THAT SAME MORNING BANDA was in line in front of the inspectors to whose knives he was supposed to submit his two hundred kilos of cacao before he would be allowed to sell to the Greeks.

The inspectors were two boys who were neither old nor young; their expression didn't reveal whether they were well or poorly fed. It must have been rather poorly given the way they behaved. They had begun by having people wait for them the better part of the morning. When they finally did arrive, they slowly reviewed the queue of people waiting for them. This little ritual took more time. Whenever they spotted a man or woman not perfectly in line, who stood out, they surmised that that person had cheated.

"Go to the back of the line. That'll teach you to be in a hurry. When you arrive, you're supposed to go to the back of the line. Will you ever get that idea into your thick bushman skull? We don't like disorder; what the devil, we don't like it when things are a mess! Don't make us call the police . . ."

They uttered these lines each time they sent someone to the back! One of the inspectors was talkative. The other didn't say a word, and rumor had it that he was the rougher of the two.

While they looked the queue over, half a dozen toughs accompanied them; there were an additional eight members of the regional guard in khaki uniforms who had been assigned to keep order. There were two lines, one on either sidewalk, getting longer by the minute. Farmers kept arriving. The men carried large loads on their heads: a half-full bag; their necks were arched, slightly straight, their back and shoulders rounded. The women carried baskets on their backs: they walked leaning forward. You could see the straps of the baskets biting into their shoulders.

With one for each queue, the inspectors worked quickly now. Frequent disruptions shook the crowd along each sidewalk, sending a momentary quiver of anxiety and confusion through the assembly. On the road that led through the two lines, pedestrians and cars kept moving along: a voluminous cloud of dust lingered in the air.

Despite the inspectors' precipitation, the queues kept growing. Pushing and shoving disrupted the crowd; shockwaves passed through the line, running either back to front or front to back. It often happened that a young man, unhappy to find himself at the end of the line, would create a better spot for himself, usually with his fists. If his adversaries thought they were in the right, and if they stuck together, they won the argument. Unless the regional guards intervened; then, the delinquent's cacao was simply confiscated by the guards. Despite this risk, young men regularly cut in from the back; with an eagle eye, they looked for a weak spot; when they found it, they pushed their way in suddenly and dropped their load between their legs. This urge to conquer happened more frequently. Eventually, there came a time when their efforts met no resistance at all; their insistence on maintaining their assaults had discouraged everyone. The overwhelmed regional guards were reduced to the unenviable role of impotent spectators who promised to intervene when it became possible.

When calm finally returned, all of the young men had succeeded in violently staking out new spots farther up the line.

I should not have come on a Saturday, Banda mused. These crowds . . . I shouldn't have come on a Saturday. In his mind, without exactly knowing why, he associated Saturday with happiness and relaxation. That's why he had thought to come on this particular day . . .

He couldn't make out what was happening ahead of him. He had to move forward constantly, only to be pushed back. As always, he took things in stride. He could feel the pins and needles in his feet.

To get his mind off the present, he began looking at the inspections that were happening on the other sidewalk. The inspector was leaning over a large wooden contraption, shaped like a cone standing on its tip. This instrument was rough; it looked as if it had been carved with an axe, poorly finished, without the slightest concern for aesthetics. It was closed at the small end by a piece of wood. It was held up between two rickety sawhorses: the whole apparatus came up to the waist of "Monsieur l'Inspecteur," as he liked to be addressed.

The cacao was transferred from the bag or backpack into the wooden object. The inspector ran his hands through the beans, which he examined for quality using a remarkably diverse array of techniques. He could, for example, press the beans vigorously in his hands: if they cracked, he stayed impassive; otherwise you were good for a few days of basking in the sun. What the devil? You didn't bring in properly dried cacao? Unless, of course . . . One way or another, he wound up splitting the beans in order to see if they contained any mold. Finally, he discretely pronounced his verdict, always with the degree of detachment appropriate to a "Monsieur l'Inspecteur." After which, he pulled away the little wooden flange thereby releasing the beans back into the bag or basket.

Officially—there existed three possibilities:

1. You were immediately authorized to sell your cacao.
2. You were ordered to dry it in the sun for one, two, or three days under the Inspection Service's watchful eye.

3. It was thrown onto the fire if its quality was far too poor for export.

In reality, there was a fourth exchange-based solution: one Banda would have done well to know about. This all looked a little too easy, he thought. Without really paying it any heed, he felt a vague sense of foreboding. Why did the inspection agent have that pinched and reticent expression?

He wasn't aware that malevolence was a tradition among these gentlemen of the control service. At the time of this tale, they were just beginning their rampage. Until that time, the quality of cacao had been settled between the indigenous producer and the Greek buyer. To everybody's delight, the administration had kept its distance. Then one day the administration decided to get involved in every stage of the process. Anyone with a brain could have seen it coming. It had begun with a team of parasites who spread across the countryside like a swarm of locusts. They would pop up in your village and set out to prove that your lands were poorly managed, that your cacao trees were arrayed in the wrong fashion, they were too close together; that the plants were badly selected. Then they would teach you how to do it right, in order to expand your holdings, to get you a better return, etc. After that, they made you work uselessly for weeks, chopping down your own trees, counting and recounting them, uprooting the saplings and carrying dead wood. It was better not to complain as that only brought more trouble: that they should appear useful was no laughing matter.

They lived at the village's expense during this so-called instruction. They appeared minimally interested in moving on. If you got sick of feeding them, they were the ones to invite you, where they would provide you with a feast—of your last remaining rooster. Going from one form of abuse to the next they had finally arrived at this new form of control: the inspection. Where would they stop?

That was what the peasants asked themselves. Any semblance of stability or security was gone; these people needed to stick their noses in your affairs, to control everything.

A wave of elbowing passed through the line. Banda had to bend over, brace himself against his load, so as not to fall.

"That's precisely what you shouldn't have done, Banda . . ."

He quickly turned to her and stared. Hey! She was as worried as he was. And the others? He looked at each in turn, leaning toward the road in order to get a better look at them. By gosh, he said to himself, they all look worried. Perhaps I should send three of them into the other queue? In fact, which is the harsher of the two? But he really couldn't compare them because he couldn't see what was happening in front of him. Which is the harsher of the two controllers? Ah, what the devil, it's not worth it: my cacao is good, there's no doubt about it.

"Banda, you shouldn't have . . ."

"What shouldn't I have done?" he asked, nervously, anxiously.

"You should have made a deal with him. You don't risk two hundred kilos of cacao just like that! Couldn't you have worked something out? I've already told you this. You should be less trusting; you never want to act like everyone else. I've heard that, with these inspectors, one never knows."

"My cacao's good," Banda grumbled. "I did everything they recommended. I followed their instructions. I have nothing to worry about: there's no reason. My cacao is of fine quality . . ."

He could have repeated this endlessly without actually convincing himself, and the fact was that he was starting to get scared.

"You can say what you want," Sabina answered, "you can say what you want. One doesn't risk two hundred kilos of cacao like this . . ."

What a thinker Sabina was!

"And you Regina, what do you have to say?" he asked.

Regina always had an enormous plug of tobacco in her mouth that prevented her from responding quickly. Maneuvering the plug into her right cheek, which bulged, she spat out the black juice into the gutter.

"That's true," she declared sententiously. "One doesn't risk two hundred kilos just like that: you should believe us; we're your mother's age. 'My cacao's good . . .' Do you even know what that means? One never says that beforehand: one says it afterward, when the inspectors have decided your cacao's good. Beforehand, it's nothing, neither good nor bad . . ."

Once again she spat black juice into the gutter. When asked, the third one answered:

"One doesn't risk all of one's cacao in such a foolhardy fashion, that's true. Two hundred kilos is nothing to sneeze at."

"You don't risk two hundred kilos just like that," the fourth chimed in.

"Well, we'll see," said the last one.

She would never know how much Banda appreciated that last comment.

"Last night, as we were walking, you were all singing. And now you're afraid!" said the young man with pique.

"Come on! If we're afraid, it's for you. This cacao is yours, not ours. We just helped you carry it, because your mother is sick and can't help you. As for the rest, you're on your own. You're an adult . . ."

That Sabina! All of a sudden, he felt horribly alone. He'd often felt this way, but rarely with this intensity. If something happened, he would bear the brunt of it on his own: his mother would only learn of it much later that night. He'd even prefer that his mother would never hear it; or at least that he, Banda, not have to be the one to break the news.

"Those inspectors," remarked Regina, "it looks like they're being stricter than usual. Is it an order they've received? . . ."

A violent shove from the back pushed them up against each other.

South Tanga stretched out in front of Banda: sparkling, white, red, green. It fascinated him. He found himself daydreaming about the little train smoking in the distance: its neat and narrow cars swallowed up passengers, people, like Greek children's toys.

Where were they going? To the big city on the coast, some three hundred kilometers away? Three hundred kilometers? Twelve hours in the train . . . Fort-Nègre, the big city on the coast! It must be full of tall buildings. What did the Black neighborhoods look like there? They certainly couldn't be as ugly as the ones in North Tanga. Maybe people lived large in Fort-Nègre with all the money that flowed there? Perhaps one didn't have to argue about two hundred kilos of cacao with the inspectors and the Greeks. Some even said that cacao wasn't important there. People made a ton of money doing things besides breaking open pods and fiddling with beans. And a man didn't have to pay a lot for a woman, to have a wife of one's own. A curse on the first man who forced his future son-in-law to fork out such a sum. Maybe that's where he'd go after his mother died, to Fort-Nègre. Yes, maybe that's where he'd finally wind up. First he would leave his wife in the care of his parents-in-law. He would have her come to the big city only after he had been there for a while, after he had made lots of money. He would wait for her at the station, which, he had been told, was an enormous house. Yes, he'd wait for her at the station. She wouldn't recognize him, he'd be so well dressed. He would take her into his arms and say, "Don't you recognize me anymore?" Her eyes would widen with surprise and she'd answer: "Banda, my dear husband, am I mistaken or is that you?" She wouldn't be able to control her joy. He would cross his entire neighborhood on the way to his cabin.

As he walked by, folks would salute him as a cherished acquaintance, and they would cry out, "Well! If it isn't our dear friend Banda! Where is he coming from like that?" And he'd answer, "I've mentioned my wife, haven't I? I told you she'd be here one of these days. Well, here she is!" As he touched her hand, their eyes would glow with envy. The inside of Banda's hut would be so beautiful that she would hesitate to enter: in the middle a gas lantern would be suspended from the roof over a pretty little wood table covered with a tablecloth; around it would be displayed wooden chairs and a wicker couch. There would be a cabinet standing in a corner, containing glasses, china plates, and aluminum forks and spoons. Fort-Nègre . . . He knew somebody from there. Nobody paid you any notice there, he'd said. Nobody would resent you for anything—except for the police, of course. Still, it wasn't like in Bamila or even North Tanga where the regional guards came to question you for no reason, just like that, and made you sweat for two weeks on some worksite, as had happened to Banda: one day he had been taken from Bamila, out of the blue, when he least expected it . . . Why think of that now?

The little train creaked to a start with the long, thin, shriek of a woman caught up in the spirit of singing and dancing. It disappeared behind a hedge of greenery: leaving only a smear of smoke behind. Then the cloud disappeared. The little train had left.

Banda sighed pathetically.

"It's a long wait, eh?" someone said.

You had to bend over at least once a minute and lean against someone for your load not to fall over. An exhausted woman had already collapsed into the roadway's red gravel. Rather unexpectedly, the inspector had even seemed touched by this. He had fiddled with her beans for a few seconds and had just as quickly set her free. Seeing this, the crowd had murmured in approval: this was also a call for a more general clemency, but there was little likelihood that the inspector would see it this way.

The day was ablaze with sunshine. It was hot and humid. The men were streaming with sweat. They passed their palms over their faces, waved them in the air, and then rubbed them against their shorts or their khaki pants. Their cotton shirts, when they had one, were as damp as if it had just rained: they unbuttoned them down to their navel and blew on themselves.

"Look at that. Have you ever seen so much waste?"

Banda was looking in the general direction suggested by Sabina's pointed maternal index finger. An impressive sight; a puff of thick white smoke was rising from a pile of red beans, drifting lazy circles into the sky. At the same time, a vague smell of chocolate filled the air.

The young man's gaze came to rest on an empty lot randomly carpeted with multicolored wraps, braids, covered with cacao beans. Here and there, a child, a woman, less frequently a man looked with resignation at his goods, squatting, knees against his chin, unaware of the same sun for which he was thankful, praying there wouldn't be a storm. Still, the storm would come. At which time they would gather up their "product"—as they called it—as fast as they could—to protect it from the ill effects of the rain, while remaining at the disposal of the government inspector, who enjoyed discretionary powers as to when they could leave. That's right: discretionary.

Joyous groups were distancing themselves from the inspector's apparatus. These were the only people in these parts who didn't look distressed. The men grabbed their half-full bags with both hands. Like weightlifting champions, they lifted the load above their waist, and let it come to rest on their head with a dull thud. The women, not without coquettishness, took their pack by the edges, lifted it, and rested it on their right knee. Then they took the right shoulder strap with both hands and, with a surprisingly quick twist of their waist as elegant as it was energetic, they brought the pack to rest on their back. Banda thought to himself that at least those people didn't have anything to complain about, as if he already surmised that his own fate would be different. He watched them happily direct their feet toward South Tanga. Their steps were light, despite the heavy loads weighing down their heads, necks, shoulders and backs: they walked in a whirlwind of dust: their bare feet looked like they were scarcely grazing the ground.

The sun was quickly climbing the sky's eastern wall and exhaling waves of heat. A car passed, its aged engine purring uncomfortably, the overly insistent horn proclaiming recent wealth. Banda barely turned around. Later he would try to return to this moment; it was a waste of mnemonic energy. A large black car with enormous protruding headlights, a

White man at the wheel, and a White woman seated next to him. In the future, he would have all the time in the world to try to remember this moment, because its importance would then be clear. Was the car going quickly or slowly? Was the sky crisscrossed with long and motionless streaks of clouds? Or were the dark bands of the oncoming thunderstorm already visible on the horizon? Was the wind plowing tiny furrows into the river? Were a multitude of pedestrians massed on the concrete bridge? Was that fisherman intensely clinging to the bow of his boat quietly holding his fishing line, or was he simply a stereotyped image, emerging from his previous life, simply inseparable from certain circumstances, from other sensations, from other images? This he would never know. He had barely seen the car when the ineluctable cloud of dust had already descended like a dark screen. To think that at the very moment when a tragedy that he thought for a while irreparable was about to touch him, a serendipitous event was already on its way to counterbalance it. Better yet, it had grazed him and he had barely glimpsed it.

The inspector was bellowing at the top of his lungs:

"Come on! You over there, let's go! What's going on? Do you think I'm going to spend my night here?"

The question made Banda smile, who hadn't lost his sense of humor despite his fear.

Two or three tussles broke out in the line again.

"Hey, it's my turn," Banda said to himself with a tremor.

He was just in time. The shriek of a siren rose from a distant sawmill and shot straight up into the hot, viscous air. It was almost noon.

Banda slowly emptied his bag into the wooden contraption. He couldn't take his eyes off the beans, which, as they banged against each other, sounded like someone walking across dead leaves. Did he ever love those beans! He had worked so hard to produce them, to obtain their present dryness, their perfect redness; it felt as if they had come from his own breast. Without a doubt, his cacao was good. His eyes met those of the functionary. The man plunged his arms up to his elbows into the beans. He rummaged around in them at length, pulled out a handful, pressed them several times into his hand . . . He remained silent. If you wanted dry, these beans were dry, the young man said to himself. He cast a quick triumphant glance at Sabina. The inspector had started selecting the beans one by one, without stopping, and with care; his knife sent out a shower of bean fragments. His expression was terse, his eyes narrow. Banda, who was increasingly nervous, squatted, and placed the bag at the opening of the contraption to capture the beans. He didn't rise to his feet: he was waiting, holding the bag by its edges with both hands. Above his head, the sharp snap of the beans told him the inspector wasn't done yet. He was really taking his time: that was a bad sign, Banda noted. No longer being able to bear it, he rose to his feet. Again, their eyes met. The man kept his gaze: as did Banda, though he was horribly afraid now.

"I have five other loads with me," he said, just to say something.

As soon as he had uttered the words he regretted them. He had spoken without being spoken to, just as when, in school, he had been threatened with punishment. The memory of those years of constant dissimulation and fear pained him.

"Is it the same cacao?"

"Yes . . ."

"Exactly the same?"

"Of course!"

He was aware of all the deference he owed the inspector, "Mister Inspector." Still, he spoke to him with energy on purpose, made an effort to show off; he wanted to avenge himself for having revealed his fear.

"Let's see it anyway."

For sure his cacao was good. Otherwise, why would he have said, "Let's see it anyway"?

The five women had calmly arrayed themselves around the controller and followed the whole transaction with some interest. He took a handful of beans and examined each one to the last. Sometimes he selected half a bean, sometimes a quarter.

All of a sudden Banda thought again about the sentence: "Let's see them anyway." And what if his beans were bad? This thought sent a stabbing sensation into his heart. Could his cacao actually be bad? He picked up his own handful of cacao in one of the packs and pressed the beans into the palm of his hand. As to whether they were dry, they were dry all right. So then what? Was the inside moldy? He never got the chance to answer this question. In the flash of an eye, the inspector's strongmen had grabbed the loads of cacao and were carrying them toward the smoldering mound of beans. What had the controller just said?

"This cacao's bad—very bad. Into the fire!"

Banda trembled with rage. His eyes welled with tears.

"No way," he roared, "that's false! My cacao's good!"

He leaped after the strongmen. One might have thought that the regional guards were just waiting for him to move. They converged. There was a quick and disorganized scrum. Fists appeared, billy-clubs swung. The massive body of one of the guards came crashing down. The five women who had accompanied Banda courageously tried to intervene.

"You can't fight four against one," they said. "Aren't you real men?" they said.

"We don't want to fight him," the guards said. "We're taking him to police headquarters, and that's it."

They had subdued him. They forced him to get up and they put the handcuffs on. The silent crowd directed its eyes and ears toward the young man. He had a black eye. Blood trickled down from his lip. A muffled wave of sound came toward him, as if the people were conveying their sympathy.

Instinctively, he struggled, trying to get rid of the handcuffs, until he realized that they were made of steel. He had only ever seen such an object from afar. When they had come to Bamila to take him to a worksite, they had just wrapped a rope around his waist. His vision was blurred. He was tired. He was thirsty.

The five women cried around the regional guards, begging them to forgive him. They humiliated themselves by saying that it was he, Banda, who was in the wrong, and that they would owe them his whole life if they were willing to overlook his slight lapse in judgment. Sabina even went so far as to claim that she was his mother: she asked for pity, no longer for him, but for him as her son. Didn't they have mothers?

"Teach your son to behave better," was the answer.

One of the women stepped out from the group and approached the inspector, whom she began to implore, arms outstretched, begging. She was pitiable; she inspired disgust, this woman pleading in the interest of another woman's child. She was pitiable, but she was also sublime; her attitude evoked a race of women now gone forever. At no time did the inspector deign to look in her direction.

"Stop, Regina!" Banda cried. "That's no man you're looking at. It's an animal." Banda's declaration precipitated a wave of murmuring and laughter through the crowd.

He suddenly saw the pile of beans from which smoke was billowing: he thought he could still see the inspector's strongmen pouring his beans onto the mound. This spectacular cloud of smoke appeared to Banda like a miracle, a lie: he looked in vain for the fire supposedly behind it. If it was there, it wasn't burning with a flame.

The pile of beans formed a pyramid with an enormous base, a wide body, and an insignificant peak. In any case, the fire or the smoke that was rising from it could only be touching a tiny portion of the beans. Banda would remember all of this later when he learned that the "bad cacao" was destined to a far less purifying destiny than fire: that when night fell it would be subjected to various recovery operations watched over by the control service's men.

While the regional guards were leading him to police headquarters, he felt a profound sense of frustration; this impression wasn't new to him either. He'd often experienced this: only this time it was particularly acute. It was accompanied today, as in the past, with this other impression, also magnified by the circumstances, that the great forest's protective mantle had been withdrawn forever.

He thought he had reached the bottom of human cruelty, not realizing that it was bottomless.

Bad cacao . . . Into the fire! . . . Like a chunk of rock, the words had bowled him over, were holding him down, impotent, filling him entirely.

They were in his stomach; he felt their weight viscerally.

They were in his lungs: the terror of Bamila, when he was knocked out for the first time in his life; he was trying to catch his breath and couldn't.

They were in his brain confusing its proper functioning; Banda felt as if he had arrived in a foreign country, far from his native land, far from his family.

They were in his eyes: myriad sparks flashed and blinded Banda in this universe that wasn't his.

Bad cacao . . . Into the fire!

He felt like he did that day in Bamila when he'd been hit so many times that he thought he would die.

A foreign woman passing through the village had taken him under her wing, though she was clearly uninterested in the other youngsters. These same youngsters had decided to punish Banda for showing off, for boasting—that's how they had labeled his behavior. To accomplish this they had set against him some bastard of a foreigner who was said to be as strong as a river. At least Banda had escaped from that battle victorious, though badly bruised. His opponent remained out of commission for several weeks.

He felt that today they had once again presented him with a ferocious opponent, this time with the certainty that he would go down. It was as if he had been told, "Go ahead and fight, poor boy, but don't delude yourself. It goes without saying that . . ."

He had been so full of hope this morning. Perhaps, he thought to himself, it's when one thinks that happiness is at hand that these things occur. Behind him he could hear the guard's soles crunching on the gravel road. He could hear them roaring with laughter: they had forgotten about the incident or they were taunting him. Were they taunting him? He wanted to be sure and listened carefully. They were speaking loudly in a dialect he didn't understand. It's true that they weren't from the area. They came from the North. It didn't appear for an instant that they were taunting him. Why did they always recruit them from the North? Maybe they were bigger and stronger up there? Maybe because, given how stupid they were, they were more manageable? Maybe it was simply that they weren't from the same region. Perhaps if they chose people from around here to be guards up there they would behave in the same way; they might be just as insensitive. It would be interesting to know who was recruited to maintain order in the North, where these two guys taking him in to face Mister Police Captain, a White man, came from! What was that guy going to say to him? Moron, dirty lazy nigger, pervert, monkey, asshole . . . The captain might slap him for having dared fight back against his men. Yes, he might slap him. He would make sure to keep his arms pressed against his body, because if the White man struck him Banda might strike back. He had never been able to suffer the humiliation of a slap, and it would not be the first time such a thing happened to him. But it would be all over if he struck the White man, over forever. It would be a source of sorrow for his poor mother; she was such a symbol of suffering. Yes! He would be careful when the captain slapped him, otherwise they would fight and it would be all over . . .

Before entering the captain's office, he imagined the image of his mother one last time, a poor, dark, emaciated object, a miserable, disgusting, inhuman, pitiable thing sprawled on a bamboo cot.

5

THE TAILOR HAD TURNED toward his nephew, to whom he was listening with intense admiration.

"Son," he said, "tell me again. Five women accompanied you . . ."

"Five accompanied me," Banda echoed.

"And the six of you were carrying two hundred kilos of cacao."

"Yes, two hundred kilos, no more no less."

"That's a lot."

"Yes, a lot."

"And they confiscated your cacao at the control point."

"Yes, they took it and threw it into the fire."

"That is, they pretended to."

"I don't know, but they threw it into the fire."

"I'm telling you. They pretended to."

"So be it, uncle, they pretended."

"Two hundred kilos."

"Two hundred."

"All taken."

"All of it down to the last bean."

"And you fought with them? . . ."

"That is, they beat me . . . There were four of them and they gave me a black eye."

As a sign of his disapproving surprise, the tailor slightly parted his lips and his pale undernourished tongue peeked out. His eyes were red, as if he hadn't slept in days. His head, entirely bald except for the back of his neck, shone in the sun. He was seated in front of his machine, at a loss, sad, meditative.

"Ah, Banda, my child, what a tragedy! Two hundred kilos of cacao in the fire! Has anybody witnessed anything like this before? Poor boy! How will you get married after this, I wonder? Two hundred kilos . . . A fortune. Working all year, clearing your land, trimming the cacao trees every morning . . . for what? Who would think of setting up controls . . . And the controllers. If our own chiefs had the courage, they would protest . . . Only they aren't ones to do that. They've never been able to face the White man without wanting to piss their pants. The chiefs? Bah! 'And go do this.' 'Yes commander!' 'And go tell your men that.' 'Yes, commander!' When will they answer, 'No commander!'? . . . Oh, go ahead and hold your breath: 'No, commander! My men have had enough.' Yeah, hold your breath. The chiefs . . . Bah! This idea of using inspectors . . . In the past we did what we wanted. . . . Nobody told us how to treat our cacao. And yet don't forget that people bought it at the highest price. Everything worked . . . more or less . . . at least we didn't complain. What's certain is that we could do without the inspectors. But no! Here they come. And they have to show you how it's done, and lecture you, and lie to you.

"You follow everything they say to the letter. Does that prevent them from confiscating your cacao? Not in the least. And does it prevent them from burning it, or rather, pretending to? Not in the least. I ask you, son, how can we possibly live under these conditions? One doesn't even know what tomorrow will bring . . ."

The man crouched over his machine. He was almost old: he probably had to ask other tailors to help him thread his needle. He pressed on the pedal; as he worked, unconscious protest caused him to constantly shake his head and shrug his shoulders. He suddenly stopped the pedaling and turned to his nephew.

"Do you know what they say? With the controllers, you have to grease palms. Yup, grease palms. That's what they're looking for. And then your cacao will always be the best. And it won't be sent to the fire. You won't even be asked to spend days cooking in the sun, looking after supposedly humid beans. Grease palms . . . Why didn't you try that, son? Supposedly, everybody does it. Didn't you know this?"

"My cacao was good," answered Banda without unclenching his teeth, barely enunciating. "My cacao was good. My cacao was dry, dry as kindling, uncle. It's not true; it had no mold in it. It was nothing but the finest quality. . . ."

The old man indulged him by listening. He took on a mysterious expression, hesitated, and finally said, "Your cacao was good. It was of nothing but the finest quality. Fine, son. All the more reason to grease some palms. And if you didn't have a little arrangement with them, all the more reason for them to take your cacao. Listen to me carefully, son. As you can see, I'm no longer young. I've been sitting on this porch hailing customers for the last twenty-five years. I've seen a ton of White men come and a ton of White men go. I know a few things about them! When you were a schoolboy, do you remember? When you lived with us, I would often tell you: 'Son, things are going badly; the country is going down the tubes; we can't see it yet; but just wait! We'll see it soon enough.' Well, it's here! If you don't have the strength, then you have to use your wiles. And, Banda, let me tell you, you don't have the strength. What's the point of speaking like a powerful man? Banda, you're a weakling; you might as well acknowledge it now. You are even weaker than I, your old uncle, your poor mother's eldest brother. Like the others, the inspectors do what they want. How can you resist them, son? Some have complained, and it's never been followed up. Nothing will ever happen, I'm telling you. Suppose I go to the inspection place tomorrow, just to check; there won't be the slightest trace of that smoky pile of beans. You know how beans burn, slowly, very slowly. Suppose you were to go there; there wouldn't be the slightest sign of those beans.

Where do you think they disappeared to, son, I ask you? Where do you think they went? And where do the orders come from? From on high; and everybody in Tanga knows that . . . Yet we don't say a word . . . No, son, you shouldn't have had that attitude. 'My cacao is the best.' You should have wondered, 'What can I do to assure that the controller lets me through?' You'd have been better off greasing some palms. Why be proud?"

Banda was seated on the enormous wooden chest in which the tailor piled his rags. He stared obstinately at his legs, his long, thin, dark legs, and the white canvas shoes that painfully constricted his big feet. His face was stony, tense, modest, mixed with a slightly bemused expression of ill-digested sadness.

His old uncle was one of the few people with whom he could speak openly, without any reservations. While a young schoolboy he had had no other father than this effusive and generous man, flaws that explained why, after twenty years in Tanga, the aging man still lived on the edge of poverty. Banda looked up at his uncle, who was imposing a steady rhythm on the sewing machine while his bald head rocked in cadence. Banda couldn't bear the sight of this hopelessness. He glanced away.

"Uncle," he said, "why don't you go back to the home country? You're so old and tired. Why don't you go back home to rest? You're exhausted."

His uncle stiffened, then looked into the distance.

"Son, you must think that's easy, right? You think it's easy; so does anybody who has never lived in Tanga, or any other city; they all think it's easy. Others have asked me the same thing: 'Why don't you just go back there?' They believe it's a breeze. In truth, it's not. It's been twenty-five years since I left home; twenty-five years I've been here; twenty-five years I've been doing this job. What would I do back home? What would I do there, eh? In truth, it isn't as easy as one would think. I'll bet I cash in my chips in Tanga, perhaps of disease, perhaps of hunger—especially of hunger . . .

The slow metallic churning of the machine seemed to rock them.

"Son," said the tailor, "do you know that what happened to you with the police captain is fascinating? One usually doesn't get out of there intact. Tell me again what happened?"

He was smiling broadly, flashing flawless white teeth that belied his age. For the third or fourth time, Banda began his story while his admiring uncle stared at him adoringly.

"Around noon they dragged me over there, two regional guards—they had just given me a black eye."

"Don't worry, son. A black eye's nothing. Just begin by applying a warm compress and then follow that with a cold compress. What's a black eye? Nothing. Continue, son."

"They locked me in a small room: I guess there wasn't a single White person left at the police station; they'd all gone off to eat. I must have dozed off; I'm not positive but I think I dozed off."

"How so, son?"

"I had squatted down, with my back against the wall, my legs under me, and my chin on my knees. And I must have dozed off; I was exhausted. And then I felt someone walking on my feet: it was a guard who'd found that way to wake me up. He led me before a White man."

"The police chief?"

"No, I think it must have been some ranking officer or another. I've seen the police chief in Bamila several times; he's not as big. He questioned me."

"Did you speak to him directly?"

"No, because I couldn't understand him. He was speaking much too quickly. I couldn't understand. So I recounted my story to the interpreter who translated. Still, I did make out what the White officer said at the end."

"What was that, son?"

"What he said went like this: 'God damn it! That does it. They've messed with me one too many times. I'm letting this one go.'"

"He said that, son?"

"Yes. First he looked annoyed. And then he seemed to think for a second and he came out with that."

"My God! What could that mean?" the tailor concluded. "It's pretty strange . . ."

Banda was looking at the market across the way; it consisted of a vast structure surrounded by smaller buildings all planted in the middle of a large plaza. The entire scene was sparkling with corrugated roofs that Banda could hear crackling in the sun. Because it was Saturday, the market was still crawling with people at three in the afternoon. The young man took particular pleasure in following the movements of the young women, because of their multi-hued cotton dresses. Young, old, tall, short, corpulent, or skinny, there were so many of them. From time to time he would spot one, with a red silk dress, yellow-skinned, pale, or White, with a straw hat, dark glasses, a purse, high-heeled shoes. One more Greek's concubine! he thought to himself, his mouth pursed with disgust.

He had a particular weakness for women from the bush who, based on a particular series of characteristics, were easy to identify. They wore simply cut, sober-colored cloth dresses. Their arms and legs were muscular. They hid their hair under a scarf. Sometimes a pack, now empty, was still attached to their shoulders. Their easy-going attitude also stood out. In joyous clutches, they ran from stand to stand, touching all the merchandise, turning objects over and over in their hands, asking for a price, arguing over it, and then finally buying nothing. Some of them squatted in front of a pile of bananas, of yams, or of oranges, calling out to a potential customer; they bargained with feigned anger, their mouths set in a snarl but their eyes smiling. Others patiently lined up in front of the butcher; when they had finally claimed their portion of carrion, they wandered off, shaking with peals of laughter.

Why, Banda thought, was it so difficult to find your own little woman among so many? In their faraway villages, how impatient they must have been to come into town today. For these women, dying for new and preferably strong sensations, the cacao season first meant long walks across the city, browsing the Greek's shops, getting a ration of beef, lazy conversations with the clerks and other young folks of the city, the surprise of unexpected sights. He would have so liked to take part in their joy, but he couldn't. Many men must at one point or another find themselves in a similar situation, he thought. But what was the point of telling himself this since it brought no consolation? Besides, he wasn't so sure. How many men had seen two hundred kilos of cacao thrown into the fire? Did many of them have their mothers at death's door? And besides, why always be in the camp of the unlucky, the miserable?

"It's getting late, Banda; if you want to head back to Bamila . . ."

"No uncle, not today."

"No? Why?"

"My mother, I'd have to watch her cry. No, I'm not heading back today."

"Oh, I almost thought that you'd decided to set up shop in the city."

He laughed, flashing his beautiful teeth.

"No, not as long as my mother's alive."

Banda was also making an effort to smile out of fear of being outdone. But a shadow suddenly crossed the tailor's face; it was his way of indicating that he was going to speak seriously.

"Sometimes I wonder if you wouldn't be better off moving to the city. Perhaps you would be better off here."

"I've thought about it plenty, uncle, plenty. But Tanga isn't what I think about. It's too small. I'd rather go to Fort-Nègre."

"Fort-Nègre!"

"Yes, Fort-Nègre . . . I'd rather be in Fort-Nègre."

"That's odd."

Again, the old man's gaze was lost in the distance: his eyes seemed to be caressing some unknown fairyland, whereas on his wrinkled forehead you could read the anguish of a wasted and vanished youth. For a long time he said nothing. Then he sighed.

"So," he said, changing the subject, "you aren't going to Bamila?"

"No uncle, not today. My mother . . ."

He wanted to delay having to recount the catastrophe to his old infirm mother as long as possible. The image of her sprawled on that bamboo cot, legs folded, face buried in her chest, pathetically bent, simply waiting for death, filled his thoughts. It occurred to him that, upon their return to Bamila, the women would tell her; she would cry over his mishap and all her hopes would be replaced by pain, a bottomless pain. He felt himself tearing up; he began to wipe the tears away but he checked himself. He didn't want anyone to know he was crying. He was intensely resentful of the inspector and those like him, those who with impunity could afford to inflict pain on some old woman like his mother, someone who had done nothing but suffer her whole life. A strange destiny: to always suffer. It was the inspector's fault if his mother suffered yet again. He told himself that he had to get revenge, but wondered how.

"You should go see your aunt, Banda. She's sick."

"What's the problem?"

"Hard to say, exactly, son. She's got pain throughout her body. It's age, you see."

"Are you sure it's not rheumatism, uncle? When I was living with you, my aunt already complained of these pains wracking her body. You should try taking her to the clinic . . ."

"What purpose would that serve, son? You know how it is. It's always the same story: you have to grease palms if you want people to help you. Son, you should know the truth: I don't have any money. Can't you see that they refuse to give me work? I'm too old."

He pursed his lips to show his disgust.

The sun was halfway down the other side of the sky. It must have been around four in the afternoon. Because it was Saturday, South Tanga was emptying slowly despite the late hour.

"Go ahead, son, find your aunt. I'll join you in an hour, as soon as I've finished with this . . ."

The air was getting thick. Immense, towering, grey-clad clouds were slowly building in dark monochrome columns over the corrugated iron roofs.

"Hurry son. I think there's going to be one heck of a downpour!"

"Yes, uncle, I'm on my way . . ."

Once on his feet, he had to stretch for a moment to bring his body back to life. He was lethargic; the heat was weighing him down. In fact, it was a good thing that it had decided to rain.

He walked, taking his time: his uncle's hut wasn't far; it was just beyond Moko, the first neighborhood upon entering North Tanga.

He saw people gathering at a crossroad, and mechanically went to join them. A crowd of onlookers surrounded a truck loaded with long logs. The driver, a panting little round man, was sprawled on the running board. Women from the forest, "village women," were writhing and moaning while pointing toward something under the truck. A few men, most likely from the forest as well, were hurling insults and challenging the driver while shaking their large black fists in his fat face, as he sat there shiny with sweat, expressionless. Banda, imitating the other spectators, bent down.

Only the little naked feet, the khaki shorts, the leather belt, and the remains of a white shirt revealed that it was a little boy; surrounding the double left wheels of the vehicle the head, neck, and beginning of the torso were spread out like strands of meat in a puddle of bright red blood. Fascinated, he looked at this image of horror. He had seen many road accidents in his day. But this time he couldn't imagine anything less human.

The hubbub was growing around the driver, who was still sagging on the running board. The assembly was getting more compact. The policemen couldn't make their way through the crush of bodies; they left, probably to get reinforcements. It was obvious that an act of violence was about to be committed against the driver. The latter finally rose with difficulty to his feet on the running board and spreading his arms, spoke to the crowd.

"My brothers and sisters, listen to me . . . Listen to me, please. Listen to me just for a moment . . ."

In hearing him you could tell his tongue was pasty; in addition, he kept stumbling over his words. Banda noted that his gaze was blurred, that his eyes were bright red and slightly swollen: "I should have guessed," thought the young man. "All these truck-drivers are the same, drunks!"

". . . You know me well," the driver was saying tearing up. "Think, you have seen me every day in this city where I have led my life as an honest man. I am the son of Mimboga, who you also all know in the town of Tomasi. You can tell that I didn't want this tragedy; I wasn't looking for this to happen. My brothers and sisters, think about it . . . My brothers and sisters . . ."

He spoke the local dialect well.

Even though he frequently stumbled over his words, the crowd calmed down; people were listening to him; they had even begun to pity him, especially the peasants, the village folk, who at first had been the most indignant.

"It's true," the women said, opening their eyes wide, "what he says is true. He does speak our language well. No doubt about it. He is one of our brothers. Poor man. If it isn't a sad sight!"

"Still," the men said, "what rotten luck."

And they shrugged their shoulders. The driver was certainly not the son of the man cited nor was he from the village he had named. Those from Tanga witnessing the scene weren't in the least taken in by a common routine. Not without some complicity, they didn't let anything slip.

Banda went on his way. The next scene to present itself literally sucked the air out of him. A group of young men in oily mechanics' outfits were carrying an enormous White man on their shoulders. Since there wasn't enough room for them all to participate, some were helping hold up the gigantic body by propping up their comrades' arms. Others held on to his hands and feet to keep them immobilized.

They were walking briskly or running: they were in a rush to unload this burden. They uttered terrible screams, their faces convulsed in anger, their eyes bloodshot. This group passed by Banda so closely that he could see the confusion and fear etched on the blubbery White man's face. A swarm of young boys, laughing, yelling, singing, and gesticulating, tailed the mechanics. Banda also followed them from afar just to see what was going on. He could hear that the White man was mumbling something, and he got closer so he could hear; he was curious to know what a White man says when he is afraid or in pain. But a truck had just parked close by from which emerged huge men dressed in khaki. Banda immediately recognized them as regional guards. The mechanics suddenly dropped their human load, which crashed to the pavement with a moan of surprise and pain. Having understood that they could no longer escape, the oil-smeared mechanics reflexively formed a square in order to fend of the guards. Against all expectations, the clash never took place. The guards ran to the fat White man, whom they respectfully brought to his feet, all the while saying to the mechanics in the local dialect:

"Get the hell out of here! Go away! My God, what are you waiting for!"

Without having to be asked twice, the mechanics quickly headed for the nearby forest. For their part, the little boys, now knowing they could act with impunity, stayed where they were: they didn't want to miss the end of such a fascinating game. No, they certainly didn't want to miss that. Other passers-by, of all ages, added themselves to their number.

The fat White man's skull had struck the stony roadway. He was writhing around and bleeding profusely; his blue outfit was already spotted with blood. His mouth opened and closed like a bellows. The guards surrounded him. Banda could make out, at the center of the group and calling out in a thunderous voice, the White officer who had released him earlier. He was speaking very quickly and Banda couldn't understand him any better than earlier at police headquarters, but he could surmise that he was relentlessly berating his men for having let the mechanics get away. He turned in the direction they had escaped, and considered it for a moment, pensively stroking his black beard. He must have understood that pursuing them would be useless, because he suddenly shrugged his shoulders and turned back to berating his men. And all of a sudden, he started kicking the rear ends of his Black subordinates, one by one. Laughter rose from the crowd; those men had, at one time or another, caused them misery; they weren't unhappy to see them suffer a bit. But Banda said to himself that in this case, something was amiss: for once, the guards had shown some empathy, and they were mercilessly getting their behinds kicked. At least the guards had really pulled the wool over the White police captain's eyes by using the local dialect to tell the mechanics to run for it. They had really tricked him . . . The White officer had clearly not understood a thing. Of course he hadn't understood a thing. Thankfully, the White officers weren't missionaries. A missionary would have understood—the police captain, well, he understood none of it. What did he think the guards were saying to the mechanics? Perhaps "You sons of bitches, we're really going to show you who's boss! If you have the balls, real balls, just stay where you are. Just you wait, you bunch of nothings, you cowards." Yes, that's what he thought the guards were telling the mechanics . . . What I don't understand is why the guards did that—they're usually not that nice. Why did they do that? . . . Maybe they knew the mechanics; maybe they once had shared an Africa gin with them. One doesn't forget an Africa gin nor the pals one drank it with . . . Yeah, why'd they do that, I wonder?

Lost in his thoughts, he hadn't realized that he had left South Tanga and was entering North Tanga; he was making his way into Moko, the first neighborhood of North Tanga. The vivid image was stuck in his mind; the regional guards and their police captain climbing into the truck taking with them the fat White man who continued to moan, bleed, and writhe. But a torrential rain began to fall. He left the road. Spying a hut reverberating with laughter, he went in.

SITTING ON A COT, he contemplated the rain. It was falling through rays of sunshine the clouds hadn't yet succeeded in covering. Great waves of water washed across the courtyard following their usual track as they rushed into the gutter that ran alongside the road. The entire area looked as if it were crisscrossed with silver thread being vibrated by someone.

The hut was squat but rather large. One drank corn beer there, the specialty of the house. It was a foamy, brown, generally cold concoction that could also be served hot if the customer wanted it that way. Patrons sat on bamboo or wooden cots, on stepladders, or empty boxes. To rest their glass, they had the choice between the ground and a single long table. Because the table was often too high in relation to where they were sitting, most preferred to rest it on their knees, or put it on the ground, for example, if they were dancing. They were drinking and talking in clusters of two, three, four, five, six. Most of them were men. Everybody knew everybody else in the neighborhood, as was generally the case in North Tanga. Before sitting down, each new arrival went around the room and warmly shook the hands that were extended, even those he didn't know—which was, it is true, rather rare. All those whose hands he touched questioned him, addressing him with his surname, or better yet, his first name—when he was a Christian:

"How are things?"

"So-so," he would say pursing his lips slightly.

This answer meant things were going pretty well . . . neither too well nor too bad but, you know, all in all, bearable. Hadn't everyone seen worse?

If there were some talkative soul or busybody in the room, he would ask:

"And how are affairs of the heart, buddy?"

"Well, frankly, not so good."

"What's wrong?"

"Don't worry about it. Nothing major. Little things, stuff that happens. You know how life is, nothing serious."

Most of the time, the others knew what he was so clumsily trying to hide. If it were something funny, they would all burst out laughing, with a synchronicity no doubt unique to them, supposing that this behavior still holds today—nothing could be less certain. Otherwise, they chastely lowered their eyes or turned away and didn't say another word, even though they knew exactly what was up: everything was common knowledge in North Tanga.

Thinking back to when he had been a schoolboy, Banda was at first surprised to find them so unchanged, with their false air of friendship, that home-country politeness, which they had only superficially preserved. They lost that sense of being a group, that special show of solidarity as soon as they left the drinking establishment. He soon noticed that some people put on airs, demonstrated a sense of superiority, haughtiness, even. These folks looked preoccupied when they entered, a smirk etched on their face; they sported a vague and condescending expression; these folks discriminated as to whose hand they shook; they were of few words, discreet. They were generally little shop owners who had recently made money and whose bellies were just beginning to swell.

He recognized them all. But for their part, they could blink and stare him straight in the face, but they didn't seem to know who he was. He also knew the woman who owned the bar, a fat lady, who came from the West, who was oddly

dressed, whose teeth were blackened, and who had an unc-
tuous way of presenting her wares. She presided over the
back of the hut, almost in the dark, between two enormous
kettles. In the one on the left she rinsed the glasses and
cups, and she mechanically plunged the washed containers
into the one on the right and drew them back filled with
corn beer. She never stood. As soon as Banda had entered
the room she said to him, "What would the little man like
to begin with?"

It's what she said to ascertain the size of glass you wanted: a glass, a small cup, a large cup, etc.

Banda didn't particularly feel like drinking. But it was
raining outside and it would be for a while. When rain
starts under the harsh light of a sun that the clouds haven't
covered, it takes a long time to stop. He had a little money
in his pocket. Why not drink? Perhaps it would help him
stop thinking about his mother, the inspector, the regional
guards, the police captain, the mechanics, simply to exist in
a void. Even earlier he had felt the need to know nothing,
to forget everything.

His lips barely touched the edge of the cup. He slowly
swallowed the mouthfuls of beer, taking a breath after each
gulp. He drank slowly, distractedly, his gaze lost in long silver threads of rain shining in the sun. He emptied the cup
by tilting his head back and he exhaled, opening his mouth
wide.

"Would the young man like another?"

"No!"

He wasn't going to get drunk. He wouldn't be taken in.
A moment later he could already feel an agreeable sensation permeate his body: a slight tickle, he might have said,
that coincided with the coursing of his blood, and he could
follow it. At the same time his spirits were given access to a
brighter place, a place of happiness, of hope and optimism.

Someone in the room was offering to buy the whole
place a drink that he would pay for himself, as if generally
he offered everybody a drink from someone else's purse,
thought Banda. The man passed by every customer and

asked what measure of beer he wanted. The young man knew that such offers were often meant to be reciprocated, even if this was never made explicit. Sometimes this was a call to a drinks battle that often ended in a bloody fight. He didn't have any more money than desire to fight. When his turn came, he innocently answered the man that he didn't want to drink. But the other was an ironic type.

"Ah, you don't want to drink." He smirked. "What kind of man are you that you don't want to drink with us? I've been watching you since your arrival: you don't say anything to anybody, you don't laugh and when your gaze crosses a woman's you lower your eyes. There's something about you that I don't trust. I wouldn't be surprised if you came from the seminary . . ."

Someone laughed a throaty disagreeable laugh. A woman called to Banda's interlocutor, simply using his first name. In fact, it was just a way of egging him on, as if she'd said, "Come on, go get him. Show us how strong you are. Don't chicken out, I'd never forgive you for it." The man was big and muscular, in his prime. Yet, under other circumstances, Banda would have made quick work of him. But today, after everything that had happened, the idea of fighting disgusted him.

"Tell us honestly, did you want to become a priest? Did you really consider it seriously? Did you want to renounce women, God's greatest gift?"

"Hey, shut your trap!" someone shouted. "Where did you ever hear that priests have renounced women? You're a funny one! Heh heh heh! Don't make me laugh. Heh heh heh! Ah! Hmm . . ."

"You would have liked to say mass, wouldn't you? *Dominus vobiscum* . . . and all the rest . . . *In nomine Patri* . . . *Per omnia saecula* . . ."

"No: You're wrong. I have nothing of the seminarian."

"Oh! There we go—I've got it! This time, I've got it. You sold a hundred kilos of cacao to a Greek this morning and you're spending your money, am I right? Answer me. Don't be ashamed. Tell me the truth."

Banda raised his eyes. The man's belly stretched out in front of him, at the level of his head. *I'm going to cave that thing in,* he said to himself, squeezing his fists . . . He would always wonder what held him back.

"That's not it either. Things aren't going well, that's all." Suddenly he was ashamed of having said that. The guy had calmed down.

"Still, you come from the forest, right?"

"Yes," Banda said.

"So, what happened? Did they send your cacao into the fire?"

"Yes."

"I should have guessed. Don't worry about it, little man. They do that to half the people who come in. Don't worry about it and drink with us, if just to forget. I'm not asking that you buy a round in exchange. Don't go thinking that . . ."

My God, he was persistent. Another guy, one of his friends, came and grabbed him by the hand, saying, "You have to understand! Youth these days have to avoid bad habits. They have to learn how to save their money. Otherwise, how would they get married? You have to understand where he's coming from."

"Who here is unaware that a wife costs a fortune these days?" someone let out.

"My son, my son," said someone who was clearly speaking to Banda, "do you think it's worth depriving yourself of pleasure just for a woman? I deprived myself for years just to buy my own. And do you know what she gave me in return? Not even a child!"

The room was now ringing with peals of laughter. Someone took on the previous speaker.

"Perhaps you'd do better to take a look at yourself rather than complaining about your wife . . ."

The allusion was malevolent; the reception was chilly; it clearly unsettled the mood in the room. A man rose with the clear intention of putting the conversation to rest.

"That's enough," he said. "Guys who get married know what they're doing; they have their reasons and . . . the money. For my part, if I don't get married it's because I'd rather be bitten by the less poisonous of two snakes . . ."

It wasn't that there weren't any fathers in the room, but they preferred to stay out of the conversation. They understood that these poor souls were just venting their frustrations: they had hoped for so much in coming to Tanga! They had to hold someone responsible for their failures, all the more obsessively in that they were getting older—so both the women they succeeded in marrying and those they had not were made into the scapegoats.

Outside the rain continued unabated. How long had it been pouring? The sun had set behind the curtain of forest. Night was closing in. The raindrops tapped obstinately, obsessively, against the thatch of the roof and on the road.

It was raining and night was falling ineluctably. Customers were coming and going. Though he looked for him, Banda couldn't make out the man to whom he'd been speaking earlier: he had left. An oil lamp was burning on the lone table in the middle of the room failing to fully illuminate it, and the corners remained in shadow.

'I can't go out into the rain,' Banda thought, and I can't stay here forever without doing anything. I guess I'll drink a few more cups . . .'

He had begun to drink again, without hurrying, but avidly. The more he had refrained earlier, the less he had any compunction about drinking now. By the seventh cup, he couldn't hold it any more: he exited to the veranda, went behind the hut, and spilled all the beer he had just absorbed into the night. He let out what sounded like a moan as he relieved himself. At the same time he became increasingly aware of how drunk he was, which amused him. "In fact, I hadn't wanted to drink. It's true, I'd swear to it, I didn't want to drink. It just happened, against my wishes, because of this damned rain." He was standing next to the wall listening to the light tapping of drops in the darkness. When he closed his eyes he felt as if he were being rocked by waves, the rolling of a canoe out in the currents . . .

He couldn't help thinking about the inspector, the police captain, the young mechanics, the red beans piled high, the White officer, the regional guards, the fat White man who moaned and writhed in pain, about his tired old uncle. No, he just couldn't help thinking about these things. Still, he felt as if a vast distance had robbed all these people of their consistency and that they would soon fly away like a wisp of smoke. Only one image continued to oppressively impose itself, one image moved him, left him shaking: his mother sprawled out on a bamboo cot, crying with short little breaths, shedding tears so big you might think they had emptied her out. For she must be crying at this moment: she must know, someone must have told her . . .

He had the sudden sensation that someone had sliced open his heart, which was bleeding profusely. Tears came to his own eyes. What could he do? What could he do? He couldn't let his mother suffer like this . . . No, he couldn't let her suffer like this. There had to be some way to find ten thousand francs somewhere, in a few days, say, in a week—but where? He violently bit his lip. Where to find ten thousand francs? In a few seconds, his mind sifted through all the men he had met in his life, all the places he had been, pausing on the safes and cash registers he had glimpsed. First, he had seen the cash box at the Catholic Mission . . . In a corner of their office—he had seen the cash box in the corner of their office. He could no doubt locate it by touch. Unfortunately, there was no way he could get into their office: it had to be well guarded. They had their watchmen and their dogs! You could be sure that they hadn't overlooked anything. Not to mention the fact that they all slept next to each other, in person, in the same building where the office was located . . . He then thought of the Administration's cash box. Well, what about the regional guards who stood watch? That vision put an immediate stop to the idea. The Greeks! Yes, that's it! The Greeks—were they as vigilant? He would rob a Greek. Nobody would be harmed: the Greeks were thieves. Everybody knew that! He could only hope he wouldn't get nabbed. But were they also vigilant? Stupid and illiterate—that he knew, just thieves. But they didn't look like they really knew how to defend themselves and they appeared negligent . . . He'd first make sure that was the case. He would gather information without revealing his true intentions. Besides, was he really in a rush? What the hell, he'd stay a few more days in Tanga with his uncle . . . He carefully and deliberately prepared himself. A level head! That's it, a level head . . . He would only take ten thousand francs—just ten thousand francs. Nobody would be the wiser: the Greeks are thieves, everybody knows it, and they are getting rich at our expense . . .

He suddenly realized that he wasn't entirely protected from the rain and decided to go back inside. You could hear women's voices coming from the hut now. That idea—he'd have to think about it . . . But there was also no rush. He'd think about it tonight, run the idea over in his head before going to sleep . . .

He saw that there were now as many women as men in the room. They were lively, clapping their hands and singing to a frantic beat. A man was swaying in place in the middle of the crowded room. These men and women weren't only familiar with each other; a certain intimacy clearly bound them together. They were singing in unison. It's rare, especially in the city, to see men and women singing together in such perfect accord. One could hear the masculine voices of the men rising resolutely from the depths, roaring, rising, bearing along the light and fluid voices of the women. It was a typical Saturday night scene.

"Look, just look, will you," a woman said, anxiously. "Something's happening on the other side of the street. Can you see it? Look!"

"Don't worry about it, it's the third time they've done that—it's nothing. It's of no importance. They're looking for boy named Koumé who worked for Mr. T."

The profoundly male voices were full of indifferent self-confidence. The women had quieted and were listening.

"Are you saying that the boy no longer works for Mr. T.?" someone asked.

"No. Don't you know that he's no longer there? That he's on the run? It's true that you never know anything . . ."

"Did something happen?"

"They beat up their boss, you know, the fat bald White guy. He's in bad shape, in the hospital. It's being said that the mechanics also took a substantial sum of money from Mr. T.'s cash box . . . In front of Mrs. T., who took a shot at them but missed. And they escaped. Koumé is the most wanted because he was the leader . . ."

"Come on," the dancer grumbled. "Is it really any of your business?"

They started singing again accompanied by a rhythmic clapping. The lone male dancer started moving his hips again; he wasn't following the beat; the rhythm was too fast for him. In the light of the oil lamp, you could see the sweat running down his convulsively contorting chest, while he pinched his lips together. Naked to the waist, he was wearing khaki pants; he had on canvas shoes that were so old and narrow that the last two toes on both feet had torn through the cloth; they preferred to bask in the sunshine.

The sound of the drops on the roof had faded. I'm going to leave, Banda told himself. My uncle has been home for hours, since he doesn't care about the rain. He must be wondering what happened to me. But the atmosphere of the room suited all these people excited by the corn beer. He didn't leave, despite his resolution . . . He should think about this idea. It was a good one, no doubt about it—he'd think about it.

On the other side of the street, the regional guards were methodically searching the houses. They held hurricane lamps at arms length: most noticeable were the big black galoshes they must have put on because of the rain—they usually went barefoot—as well as the grim puttees that wound around their thin legs. It was the third time that they had searched the area to no avail! After a while, they reformed their ranks and headed back toward South Tanga. Pensive, Banda watched them move away.

He would have to think about this idea . . . The Greeks, a race of thieves . . . There wouldn't be anything wrong with that. All sorts of memories came back to him: his catechism classes . . . if you steal one franc from an old woman who has only that to her name—grave sin. Mortal sin. Whereas if you steal one hundred thousand francs from a millionaire, you may not even be committing a venial sin. Yeah! One hundred thousand francs—that was serious money! He would only take ten thousand . . . That boy, Koumé, must be an incredible man. If he could meet him, perhaps he would show him the ropes. Perhaps the guards would search his uncle's place? They wouldn't find me, but, of course, they would find my uncle . . . What would they do to him? They might mistreat him. When they can't get the guilty party, they always take it out on his family, on his friends . . . It's a sure thing that they'd mistreat him. My uncle—he's very tired. He should go back to the country . . .

A young woman's outline appeared in the doorway. Banda jumped: a shiver traveled from his head to his feet. He was ashamed because of what he was thinking. "I thought it was her," whispered the young man. "How stupid! What would she be doing here? Given that she is watched over by her father like some precious merchandise, why would she have come to the city?" He hadn't thought of her all day. This realization amused him. Why, he wondered? Perhaps everything that had happened had simply not left him the time? Perhaps he was too preoccupied to worry about his mother either?

Now he was thinking intensely about that girl: to his surprise, she elicited in him a kind of disgust. As long as he told himself, "I'm going to marry her, my mother will be overjoyed," he was happy to think about her, to speak of her, to see her. But after what had happened today, he was positive he wouldn't be able to marry: as a result he found her flawed, both physically and morally. For example, he couldn't stand the kind of veneration she had for her sorcerer of a father. Tonight, he also disliked her passivity with respect to her parents, her indolence, her too constant good mood; was she always happy, had she never suffered? . . .

Hey! The young woman had taken a seat next to him on the cot. He noticed that she was casting a nervous glance about the crowd as if looking for someone. Their gazes crossed. She frowned: she was ashamed that she appeared to be looking for a man.

"Are you trying to find someone?" Banda asked.

"Yes, my brother. He didn't come home. He always drinks on Saturday nights."

She was fearful, circumspect, like a crouching animal. He thought of all of the questions he would have had to answer if it had been the other girl, stupid questions: "How are you going to marry me now? You absolutely have to have the money," or "Can you wait until next year? perhaps you'll have better luck with your cacao then." Or yet again: "What do you think I should say if my father wants to marry me off to someone else? My father is growing impatient, you know . . ." He turned back to the young woman; he was surprised to find himself examining her. He felt a violent urge to speak, to confide in her: this desire told him that he was completely drunk.

"You have a funny expression. What's your name?"

"I've looked everywhere; it's getting late. I don't know where else to go."

"Don't worry. A man has never *been* a woman or a child: he doesn't get lost; he always finds his way. People must also be wondering where I am. But look, I'm fine, aren't I? No, a man never gets lost, he always finds his way . . ."

"Perhaps he drank and can't get himself home without someone's help?"

"Perhaps he has problems that he doesn't want to tell you about . . ."

"I live alone with him . . ."

"Well, perhaps you ask too many questions. And tonight he simply doesn't feel like answering them. Sometimes, one can't go home for that simple reason. Just between us, that's my case."

"You have problems?"

"Oh! Yes . . ."

He sighed. He vaguely told her about his trials and tribulations, laying particular stress on the black eye, the only visible sign of what had happened. He spoke about the other girl without emotion. Modesty prevented him from mentioning his mother. She seemed particularly intrigued. When he was done, she visibly relaxed: she looked much more at ease now.

"People still pay to marry a woman where you're from?"

"Oh yes, lots. So much that I have known men who worked for years to save enough to get married. For years, they've done everything possible to make enough . . . After the death of my father, I at least was lucky enough to inherit a plantation, though not a large one, mind you. But what's the use? They took my cacao and gave me a black eye on top of that. So where you're from you don't have to pay?"

"No, that's over. The whole tribe got together one fine morning. They spoke for a long time. There was a chief, a Black priest from the region, and a White man, an administrative officer. They decided that it was over, that they would no longer sell their daughters like cattle. But it doesn't really solve that much. My brother will still have to pay because he wants to marry a girl who isn't from my area. I know they'll make him pay. Then what?"

"Those in my hometown got together as well, but it yielded nothing. They all have daughters that they hope to sell one day. They told the White priest and the administrative officer that they would never give up a tradition passed down to them by their ancestors. The White people answered that they were mistaken: it wasn't at all a tradition passed down to them by their ancestors, etc. The White men didn't insist because around our parts, discussions with strangers aren't particularly welcome, and there was a chance that it could end badly . . . Do you ever drink beer?"

"Yes, if you want to offer me some."

She had hesitated a bit. It was in the order of things. Unconsciously, he was delighted to have stayed a little longer at the precise moment when he thought that this young woman was uninterested in him; in any given week, one has many encounters like this as long you're willing to stay in the city.

They drank. They were seated side by side, quietly meditating, in the midst of people who were singing and clapping and who, between songs, made suggestive comments. He took a half pack of cigarettes from his pocket; they were crumpled; they had spent the entire day in his pocket and he had forgotten about them.

"Do you ever smoke?"

"Never!"

"That's odd: I thought that all city women smoked."

She looked up, her eyes watery. Banda did note a glow in the young woman's eyes; but he didn't figure out immediately that it was a tear. He was hungrily breathing in the smoke, without giving himself time to breathe. How could he have forgotten to smoke for an entire day? He must have been really upset!

"I'm not from the city, that's where you're mistaken."

"How so?"

She clearly didn't want to answer. But a young woman must always say what tribe she is from, what her clan-name is, where she was born, at the risk of making a bad first impression.

"I've only lived in Tanga a few weeks, three to be precise. I was born in Zamko, far, very far from here . . ."

He now understood why she was so timid. It's true that she wasn't a city woman yet. He felt a growing sympathy for her. He even forgot, now that he had confided in her, to think about his plan. A good idea, no doubt . . . Nobody would get hurt, in fact. The Greeks were thieves, weren't they? He'd get information; yes, he'd get it . . . When he came back to her, he began to devour her with his eyes, finding her very beautiful, but this didn't impress him that much—he knew that when he was drunk he tended to find all women beautiful just because he wanted them. She sighed.

"I also have problems," she whispered.

"Really?"

"Yes, I have problems . . ."

"Don't worry about your brother; it's really not worth it, believe me."

She looked at him with surprise, and then her apparent astonishment disappeared just as quickly.

"I swear . . . I have problems."

"Serious ones?"

"Very serious, life and death."

"Tell me. I'll help you: I can assure you that I'll help. Tell me, you'll see, I'll help."

He wasn't just saying it, he believed it. It was a reflex: he couldn't witness suffering without vibrating at the same wavelength as the person experiencing it. It was something he couldn't control.

"I lied to you earlier," she confessed. "I wasn't looking for my brother, but an old woman friend to ask her advice, and to have her look after our hut in case I suddenly have to leave Tanga."

"Why?"

"My brother was a mechanic at T.'s place . . . The guy who has a sawmill near the river." She was speaking in a low whisper.

"His name was Koumé . . ."

"You know?" She drew herself up.

"I just heard about it."

They looked at each other for a moment. Outside, night had completely fallen, thick and sticky; the rain had become so fine that the drops were imperceptible.

"They are looking for him."

"Yes."

"I suppose he must be far from here at this hour."

She didn't answer. She remained curled up on the bed, fearful, panicky, like a tracked animal. She came closer to him; their bodies now touched. She was wearing a light cotton dress through which he could feel her radiant femininity vibrating. God, she was scalding hot! Banda felt like screaming; where she touched him was scorching. He didn't move. In reality, this girl was like so many others; it was just that he was drunk. She leveled an ardently inquisitive gaze at him. He could make out her beautiful face by the light of the oil lamp. She was looking him over. He took her hand. It didn't happen often, but without knowing why, he had taken her hand.

"What's your name?"

"Banda. And you?"

"Odilia."

"How odd! My younger sister had the same name. She was beautiful . . . Just like you . . ."

"Did she die?"

"Yes, very young. She was only a little girl. She just died one day: she had barely been ill."

"Did you really love her?"

"Oh, yes. You wouldn't believe how much I miss her."

Later he'd admit that he hadn't wanted to lie, that he didn't know why he had told her this entirely made up story. He only knew one thing: he had always wanted a younger sister and sometimes it felt as if he indeed had had one who had died young. He couldn't have said where this impression came from, but he had it often. That was the simple truth. The interesting thing is that he had always given this imaginary sister the name Odilia. That too was the simple truth.

He was pressing her hand softly. He wanted her. At least this one wasn't a used up woman, she wasn't someone who had been manhandled, pressed to a pulp like a lemon, or polluted by alcohol. He could feel that she was fresh and young. He had forgotten his idea, his great idea, as well as the Greeks, that race of thieves.

"Where were you born?"

"In Bamila, not far from here on the southern road."

"Yes, I know where that is."

"You can speak to me without worrying."

"You're drunk."

"Yes, I've drunk a bit, true. But I'm not drunk. No, that I'm not."

They were quiet for a second.

"Can you help me?"

"Of course, little sister, of course. Tell me everything. Don't be afraid. Do I look like a traitor? Look at me carefully and tell me, do I have that appearance? Could anybody be mean to you, Odilia? Speak to me . . ."

So something was that urgent, that serious? So be it. He would help her anyway. It would be like doing something for his "dead little sister." Besides, more than anything else, he wasn't in the habit of sleeping with virgins. The other one was also very young. But with her it was about marriage, and marriage was a whole different story . . .

She brought her lips close to Banda's ear: "I'll tell you where my brother is. He's hiding in the bush—the nearby bush. Not far from the hut where we used to live. He's afraid . . . He could be caught at any moment—they are searching for him. He came back to tell me to leave and was trapped; there are roadblocks everywhere, at least one on every path. The White man in the hospital. They say he has a fractured skull—perhaps he'll die?"

She had spilled this all out in a steady stream. She stopped and sighed. She was pitiable. She must really love her brother! He *should* have a little sister just like this young girl who vibrated with love for her brother. He was moved.

"They mustn't catch him," Banda whispered, terrified. "They'd kill him immediately . . ."

"They would kill him on the spot, no doubt."

"They must not find him."

"I'm telling you that if they catch him, they'll kill him on the spot."

"There is no doubt that that they would kill him."

He nervously squeezed her hand. She didn't understand that it was out of nervousness. All of a sudden she was afraid, and protesting while pulling away. Her mouth was pinched:

"Leave that alone," she moaned, almost in tears. "It's only for my brother that I was asking you to help me; if they find him, they might kill him."

"Who told you that he can't get past the roadblocks?"

"Do you think he can?"

"Of course. Through the woods! There are trails that are rarely traveled, and shortcuts as well. I know the region like the back of my hand. I went to school up there, you know? And the police consist only of foreigners who don't know the lay of the land. They can't set up roadblocks in the forest. They can only put them on the roads and paths that are regularly traveled, the ones they're familiar with. They're afraid of the forest the way you would be of the ocean: there aren't any forests where they come from. Travelling on known roads and trails is out of the question, but the forest is more or less foolproof. And I know all the trails in the forest . . ."

"Banda," she said in a voice that expressed an almost irresistible ardor, "help my brother; help him. He's more or less your age—it's almost like he's your brother. He was alone here and I've only been here for a while. He knew almost nobody—he only had friends in the workshop . . . A strange boy, always gloomy and alone. Help him, I beg you. Wouldn't you like to be my brother as well?"

"No, I'd rather be something else," he said maliciously . . .

And then suddenly more seriously:

"But I'm going to help your brother, you'll see. I'm going to help him. They got me, they even gave me a black eye, and I swear, they won't get him. At least they won't get him."

IT WAS DARK OUT. You could hear the faint drip of the drizzle on the humid ground. From time to time, Banda stepped into a puddle and the muddy water splashed him up to the knees: it ran back down, cold, tickling the length of his legs, and worked its way into his canvas shoes. The latter made an oily sound, like a short snore. He wondered what these shoes were good for now, since he had donned them for what he thought would be a party. Instead, it had turned into a grim journey that was ending in a dangerous adventure. He had cleaned and bleached them only a few days ago. The same day he had also washed and ironed his khaki shorts and the blue short-sleeved shirt that he was now wearing. When he had done those things he was still whistling and singing and laughing . . .

He stopped, bent over: without having unlaced them, with a nervous, angry gesture, he tore off the canvas shoes, one after the other. He felt more at ease once his feet were free. He walked faster and with a more assured step.

He had a hard time following the young woman whom he couldn't see.

"You did the right thing," she murmured.

"What right thing?"

"Taking off your shoes."

"Why didn't you tell me to take them off?"

"I was waiting for you to think of it yourself . . ."

What a funny girl! It's true that what he should have had was a loving sister like that: he would have felt less alone. There's no doubt: he should have had a loving, devoted little sister just like that.

They were going through various neighborhoods. They preferred to worm their way among the huts thereby avoiding encountering anybody: such a person would have asked questions. I'll go live in Fort-Nègre, thought Banda. I won't spend my time rolling around in Tanga's mud. That's for sure. He was disgusted by the ugliness and misery of North Tanga, with its squat, insignificant, poorly constructed huts, peppered with holes that revealed what was going on inside. Here a man and woman were arguing or fighting, there a child was being beaten, a baby was getting a colonic, a phonograph was howling. Farther along, drinkers filled up a space to the point where one wondered how it kept from simply flying away, so many piercing voices filled it . . . They avoided the street for fear of being surprised from behind . . . A heavy smell of latrines hung in the air.

"Over here!" she said, crossing the street.

He admired this kid's courage and precision. How would the other girl have dealt with these circumstances? He felt tremendous pity for Odilia, alone among so many indifferent and cruel people, among so many dangers and traps, alone and so far from her parents. He suddenly realized that what he disliked most about the other girl was that she let herself be babied by her father—a sorcerer—and by her mother, like an egg or a chick. He felt closer to Odilia, as if they were on the same level: she was alone now, as alone as he was. By the way, was he going to see Koumé? He might ask him for a lead on his business, his big idea—a Greek, just swipe ten thousand . . . Nothing more. Nobody gets hurt . . . But when would he pull it off? He had promised to help Koumé; he'd probably hide him in Bamila. Too bad! He wouldn't be able to pull off his job. Hey, why not? Weeks, months later—yes, that's what he would do. He would first make sure that Koumé was safe, then one of these days, in Bamila he would ask him for a lead, as if he were just kidding. And perhaps he would burst out laughing, and say, "Hah! A Greek, what could be easier?" Yes, that's what he would say . . . He would wait for him to be safe in Bamila then ask him for that lead, as if he were joking.

In the meantime, he had forgotten all about his mother! The outdoors and fresh air had given him back his courage, his motivation. The corn beer, for its part, continued to operate, particularly in his eyes: it wasn't uncomfortable, rather the contrary. It helped transform reality, just enough not to feel too sad. It was one of those strange things in life . . .

He didn't have the leisure of pursuing his meditations. They were quietly entering a small, narrow hut. Banda struck a match, but Odilia just as quickly blew it out.

"We're lucky that it's this dark out tonight. Don't get us caught," she said in lieu of a reproach.

Then she touched his arm.

"Stay here. I'm going to call him. It would be better if you didn't light another match."

Now alone, Banda looked into the darkness. He could see nothing but the gloom, great swaths of black, nebulous forms, flows and spirals of granular, fleshy, spongy darkness. He wouldn't have been able to make out a man more than three feet away. What will we do in the forest? he wondered. Would they bring a torch, an ember, something with which to see? No, it would be better to bring nothing: something like a torch or ember would only signal their presence. He knew the forest well enough to be able to navigate it at night without needing a light. All of a sudden, his thoughts turned to the regional guards. Perhaps they are posted around the hut? Perhaps they're waiting for Koumé to enter in order to jump on him? If they came along, what would he do? Without thinking, without hesitating, he knew. He would fight with rage, like a madman. With them, Banda felt that all he could do was fight, send his fist into their faces, get punched by them in turn, punch back, struggle . . . He would clear a path with his fists and he would escape into the forest. If he got caught, they wouldn't spare him either. A multitude of images swirled in his mind:

"Bah! A Greek, could anyone be easier to rob?" Yes, there's no doubt that that's what Koumé would tell him tomorrow or one of these days in Bamila, and he'd say it while laughing; he, Banda, would also laugh, to stay in the same mood, to make it appear that it wasn't for himself that he was asking. They would both laugh out loud . . . Odilia, smiling, would look at both of them with admiration. He would tell the story of the guy who oversaw a Greek's shop: he had done the accounting in a single ledger that he had then burned, which in turn allowed him to rob the Greek of as much as he wanted. In the end, the Greek and the man found themselves in front of a courtroom, a courtroom of White people, French people. They said the following to the Greek: "Really, you dishonor your race. Ah! What an idiot you are! How could you get scammed in this way by a native?" The Greek of course couldn't check anything because the account book had been burned . . . They would all laugh . . . It was a true story which he would only tell not to be outdone by Koumé if he started berating the Greeks . . . Who didn't know this story?

With the stealth of a cat, a shadow slipped noiselessly into the hut: it was the girl. Another shadow followed: just as discreetly. The man seemed big to Banda as he stood opposite him. They sized each other up in the darkness with neither really seeing the other. What must this Koumé, this tough guy, look like? Banda wondered. A gust of wind rushed through the little door bringing with it a penetrating coolness.

"We have to hurry," Banda worried. "They can come at any time."

"Who?" Koumé said.

"Who? The guys from the regional guard, of course; didn't anybody tell you? They have done nothing but search in the Black quarters. They search one hut they suspect and then leave. Later they come back and search another. Odilia, why didn't you tell him?"

"We could only communicate sporadically. Besides, wouldn't he have taken fright?"

"Are there Whites with them?" Koumé asked.

"No!"

"Then there is nothing to be afraid of. The Blacks are searching just to keep up appearances. What worries me is if there are Whites at the roadblocks. If there are only Blacks . . ."

"Are you joking?" Banda worried. "If there are only Blacks, you say . . . The younger ones, I can't say, perhaps they do something nice from time to time—they let you run away this afternoon. But the older ones are a different story—they want to advance in rank, and since they are illiterate, the Whites count on their docility . . ."

"Were you there, this afternoon?"

"Yes I was, and I saw you; you're all very brave. If there were nothing but people like you, those like T. would be rare."

They were silent for a moment.

"What are we going to do? We should hurry."

Koumé's teeth were chattering and he was trembling: you could tell by the choppiness of his breathing. Was he afraid, or had he spent too much time in the rain and cold? Banda thought it must be both.

"Are you afraid?" he asked the young man.

The question unsettled Koumé and must have even hurt his feelings. He answered without unclenching his teeth. Was he afraid? Why ask? And what would be the use of being or not being afraid? And wouldn't anybody be afraid? A White man was going to die and he, Koumé, was the one they were going to accuse. Right? He had to ask if that, being accused of killing a White man, wasn't something to be afraid of . . .

Banda was listening to Odilia's brother: he liked his voice as well as his personality. He wondered why . . . Perhaps it was because he was Odilia's brother, someone who had been given a little sister the likes of which he had only dreamed. Perhaps because he had always dreamed of seeing this type of boy, a "tough," as they were called. Of course, without his mother, he himself was a tough. Perhaps also, it was because he reminded him of an old school friend from up there. Whatever it was, he noted that he liked Koumé, and it was rare that he liked a boy that much. He felt the sense of kinship that he had with Odilia slowly include her brother.

"Don't get your feelings hurt, trust me," Banda said, putting his hand on his shoulder.

He felt him jump, stiffen, and then back off slightly. Was he going to hit him? He closed his eyes, scowled, and waited for the blow somewhere on his face, but nothing happened. Koumé had simply backed away.

"Don't be afraid, old man," Banda said in a confident tone and with emotion. "Don't be afraid. If there is a man who wants to turn you over to the regional guards, it's not me. I assure you, I'm not that person. They owned me this morning: after taking my cacao, they almost got me thrown in prison. To think that they had already beaten me up. They even gave me a black eye . . ."

He was silent for a moment, he was panting slightly, and then he began speaking again:

"Besides, in my country, and especially in Bamila where I was born, people have all sorts of faults but they never turn anybody in to the Whites."

The other man had relaxed. Who had not heard of Bamila? A ferocious town in a ferocious country whose population could claim several murders of all types of representatives of law and order, whether regional guards or territorial guards.

"I can't allow myself to be captured, they would kill me on the spot," he explained.

As if he felt that weren't enough, he added, after a short pause:

". . . I am my parents' only son."

"I understand that," Banda said. "They probably only set up their roadblocks on the main roads and trails. I know because this isn't the first time . . . The forest is clear. I'm going to lead you to my village, six to ten kilometers from here by the southern road. I'll hide you there until you have some idea of where you want to go next. But please, let's go quickly, they could be back at any minute."

"Will we have to cross the river?"

"Without a doubt."

"In a canoe?"

"Would you rather cross it on the bridge?"

"Aren't you afraid?"

"What?"

"A canoe with the river at flood level?"

"I'm used to it."

"Have you crossed it often?"

"Yes."

"In a canoe?"

"And even swimming. Haven't you?"

"Never. How many times?"

"I can't count them."

"How many times swimming?"

"I don't remember."

"Are you crazy?"

"No. Don't you know how to swim?"

"It's not my fault, there are no rivers where I come from. Are you also taking my sister?"

"What else would we do with her?"

What a strange boy, Banda thought. Why hasn't he learned how to swim since arriving in Tanga? It's true that one doesn't learn to swim alone. He heard Odilia sobbing.

"What's going on?" Banda worried. "We should have left already. Why is she crying now?"

Koumé explained that his sister was sad because she had to abandon her kitchen utensils and such.

"Still, she can't stay here and she can't take that mess with her. For one, they would torture her to make her talk, and for another all those things would slow us down if we were pursued."

"You're right," agreed Banda.

He turned to her and said, "Listen, little sister. Don't worry. Some day we will come back and pick up all this stuff, you and me, I promise. Just take your clothes; one of these days, we'll come back for the rest. Just trust me."

Just trust me. How he liked saying that to people! How he liked people trusting him! Then he felt himself grow in height until he was as tall as that palm tree whose outline you could make out against the darkness. At such times, he could have accomplished anything to justify that confidence. He had noticed that in the city people gave tremendous importance to money, to riches, or to those who had them: that irritated him. Is having money everything? He didn't have any and would have been very happy to get some. Still, it wasn't everything . . . By the way, would this boy give him the lead he wanted? He didn't know how to swim . . . How can you not know how to swim? A man like that should know how to swim . . . It's not that hard. True, it's not his fault . . . no rivers where he lives. Strange boy but nice, very nice, and his sister . . . He's a lucky guy . . .

The night under the tall trees was not as dark as Banda had feared: its thickness had greatly diminished, and the moon wasn't far away. They had taken a path that was difficult to follow. You could tell it was infrequently, very infrequently, traveled: only those in the know could have been aware of its existence. The vegetation hid it almost entirely. They advanced slowly, by touch, noiselessly.

Banda led the way and guided his two friends. The young girl followed him closely. Behind her, Koumé kept turning around as if a regional guard were silently tailing them. They had to push apart the branches that blocked the path and constantly whipped their faces. They didn't speak. Since they couldn't see each other, they touched often. It must have stopped raining, but water dripped steadily from the trees, it might as well have been raining. Occasionally, a gust of wind shook the towering and distant treetops and they could hear the drops of water crackle like a steady stream of curses. Although all three of them were used to the forest, to its writhing, mysterious, dark, existence, they stopped often to make sure that they were truly alone, that

there were no intruders. They were soaked: the water was
dripping down their cheeks, their necks, and their backs.
They listened for their own footsteps, but their bare feet
on the trail made no noise, covered as they were by the
sound of drops on the tree leaves, and on the dead leaves
that sometimes remained dry despite the rainwater covering the ground.

"We're far from the city now," Banda declared. "You can
speak if you want to. They won't look for you here."

Koumé was suspicious of their guide's confidence. Who
was this boy, anyway? Wasn't he drunk? Had circumstances
sobered him up?

"What happened exactly?" Banda asked. "Tell me, what
happened? Koumé, I'm asking you."

Here we go. He was going to do something to shut him
up. He wondered what it would be. "Can you shut your big
fat ass of a mouth?" That's what he was going to say. But
all of a sudden, Koumé realized that they were skirting the
river. He watched it flow slowly like a vast black serpent, silent, shiny, majestic, terrible. It's true, the city was far away;
he could speak. He sighed . . .

"Judge for yourself: that pig didn't want to pay us . . . I
wonder what he was thinking. That we live in his stomach,
perhaps . . . All he has to do is eat and we're fed as well? The
bastard! He hadn't even paid us for last month and we're the
thirteenth today, right? Well, he always devised some way
to send us away each time we demanded to be paid. Yesterday we'd had enough, so we went to explain all this to the
police captain, who promised to speak to him. But what do
you expect those two to talk about? I ask you. They are as
tight as the finger and the nail. It's even said that they exchange wives—it wouldn't surprise me. This morning, they
must have drunk whisky instead of discussing us. Mr. T.
was extremely excited when he returned from his visit with
the police captain, so he gathered us together. He's the boss
and we are the workers—that's what he told us. He com-
mands, we obey, and that's it. It wasn't wise on our part to

go blabbing about him to the authorities. We had to understand that the authorities couldn't force him to do anything. We had been insolent and he was deferring our pay another few days just to show us how to behave—that's what he said. Except that this time we had decided that we weren't going to let him walk all over us. At noon, once we had left the workshop, we hatched our little plan. We'd force him to come with us to the police commissioner's office and then he'd have to pay us—we really believed this. It was over between him and us; we wouldn't work for him anymore. This afternoon, when he realized what we wanted to do he fought like the devil. We nevertheless succeeded in carrying him on our shoulders. I wonder if his wife was the one who called the police . . . I never would have thought that lazy woman capable of reacting so quickly! She was upstairs, probably sleeping—I think the ruckus must have frightened her, so she sent her houseboy to get the police. They came with the White officer to stop us. You didn't have to be Jesus Christ to figure out how they were going to react. We dropped that fat T.—thinking we were going to have to fight, but the guards preferred to have us run."

Later, when Banda tried to evoke this man who had been his friend for only a few hours, he'd have a hard time making out Koumé's shadow, at night, in the midst of the forest crackling with raindrops . . . Banda's ears would always hum with his voice telling this story, with its strange inflexions.

A wild party of moonlight animated the canopy of tightly woven leafy treetops: crumbs of dim light dotted the ground and the shrubbery, hung onto the tree trunks in pale round little disks. He couldn't see the river any more: the path must have moved away from it momentarily. Only a low, heavy rumble gave away its crushing presence.

"And the money?" Banda asked suddenly.

"The money? What money?"

"They say you stole it."

"We didn't steal anything."

"The woman shot at you."

"We only went back to the workshop to pick up things that belonged to us: we weren't stealing anything. She fired, that's true. But only because she was afraid . . . She was afraid. I don't know what she thought might happen, but she was afraid so she fired. In any case, nobody was hit . . ."

Banda wondered if he was lying. If the money belonged to them because they hadn't been paid, then he was right: they were just picking it up, not stealing it. That's it, they simply recovered it—they believed it was theirs. Hey, they were right . . .

"Where are the others?"

"How should I know? We all took off in different directions . . ."

Banda stopped, turned half around, grabbed the young girl's hand:

"You, Koumé, stay here. I'm first going to lead your sister. When I'm on the other side I'll strike a match and that way you'll be able to see the walkway. It's a tree trunk full of holes and bumps and it's extremely dangerous. So stay here and don't move. When I strike a match, you'll be able to come; not before, be careful . . ."

He stepped onto the walkway holding Odilia, who followed behind him, by one hand. He was moving with care, at a pace worthy of the slowest tortoise.

"Don't be afraid, little sister. If you slip just brace yourself against me."

Under them, the water was howling against the rocks. The last rain had swollen the stream; it was soiling the river with water that the moonlight revealed was heavy with mud. Banda didn't stop encouraging Odilia.

"No point in trembling, little sister. We're almost there."

At the same moment, a violent shock accompanied by a dull thud shook the walkway. You could hear a loud splash at about the same time.

Just as quickly, Banda realized that he was flat on his stomach on the high bank; his right hand held Odilia under the armpit, which prevented her from falling in. She was

desperately clinging to the riverbank that she was hope-
lessly trying to climb—the rise was sharp, perpendicular.
Banda absorbed all this in a flash. Odilia had been frightened in hearing the splash. Had she been startled or had she
turned around? In any case, she had fallen. Luckily, he had
already gotten one foot on the level part of the riverbank.
How had he succeeded in grabbing her by the armpit? My
God! If she'd fallen, she would have fractured her skull on
the stones below! My God, if she'd fallen . . . But then, Koumé! This discovery almost led him to cry out, but he didn't
have the time because he was struggling. Yes, he had been
struggling for a while and had only just now realized it. His
stomach was slipping on the wet ground and rain damp-
ened dead leaves. Darn! The young woman's weight was
dragging him irresistibly, almost imperceptibly. She made
one last effort to hang on. He felt her go stiff, heard her
moan. A chunk of soil gave way, further accentuating the
steepness of the incline. That was all they needed! She was
now dangling in the void. She was going to fall, he could
not let her go for an instant . . . She was dragging him down
irresistibly, imperceptibly—they were going to fall for sure,
both of them, into the rapids where they were both going to
bash their skulls against the rocks. His arm was in horrible
pain. What to do?

Ah yes! He was still holding the girl under the arm. She
was moaning; her shoulder must be in pain. What to do?
Unh! He must be close to death, this is what it must feel like
. . . His left hand, ferociously gripping the ground, rubbed
against a sapling and clung to it furiously. And if the sapling
gave way? No—it wouldn't. It might if he pulled too hard.
Now what should he do? He had only succeeded in halting
their fall into the abyss. He felt a sharp pain in his right arm.
He wanted to scream, to cry: tears were blurring his sight.
Hey! Right next to him, to the left, the walkway came to an
end and was buried in the riverbank! The contortion that
took him astride the end of the walkway would astonish
him for the rest of his life. His feet were wrapped together
under the log, his heels dug into the bank. Without hesitat-

ing, he took his left arm and hooked it under Odilia's other armpit. Then he went taut, straightened out, arched himself, and pulled up . . .

He was out of breath and panting, pouring with sweat. Odilia was sobbing:

"My brother—he fell! I called out to him . . . He doesn't answer—he drowned! My brother . . . Koumé, answer me! He doesn't answer! He drowned!"

Banda thought the young woman's sobs would break his heart.

"I beg you, Odilia, don't cry like that."

For a moment it felt as if he might as well cry himself. The urge painfully constricted his throat.

Then he told himself that Koumé was perhaps not dead: all he had to do was pull him from the water immediately. That's it; he was going to pull him from the water and immediately at that. Perhaps he wasn't dead . . . But how to get to the streambed? How to get there? He was at a loss. How to get to the streambed? Yes! He knew how to get there, he had figured it out, he knew how to do it . . .

"Stay here," he said to the young girl who was still crying.

He ran like a wild man downstream, he was stumbling against saplings, he was getting tangled in bushes. Jesus! Make Koumé be still alive . . . He realized that he was praying for the first time since a priest had informed him that, because he couldn't recite his catechism properly, he wasn't ready to be baptized—it had been a long time. This memory amused him, despite the circumstances. No, Koumé could be dead for good. Why would something like that happen to him, such a courageous boy, a tough guy?

Here the stream ran at the level of the stream-bank. There was no drop. Banda was breathing quickly, and swallowing his saliva. He took his clothes off in a flash. Naked, he entered the water and began walking upstream toward the walkway. The water beat torrentially against his legs, frequently making him stagger. He could hear Odilia sobbing above him; the walkway was near. He was striding against the frigid rock and his heart was beating violently. The water poured over the stones with a moan. A large wave beat down on his legs and he staggered, like a sleepwalker, he bumped up against Koumé's cold body. He bent over, and felt around the body for a long time. Odilia, no longer crying, was leaning over:

"You've found him, haven't you? Tell me if you've found him . . . Is he dead? I want to know if my brother is dead or if he's alive. Tell me if he's dead. I want to know!"

He raised his eyes and shivered:

"Odilia, back away, please, you could fall."

She burst into tears again. She was crying harder now.

"Tell me if he's dead. Oh! Tell me."

"I can't know."

They rejoined back at the place where the embankment ended. Banda placed the soaking body on the fallen leaves. Koumé was indeed dead; his corpse was like ice. Blood that was still warm filled his mouth. A gaping wound pierced his skull at the back of his head: all around it the bone was soft.

He could have avoided this, thought Banda. All he had to do was wait for me to strike a match. To think that he could have avoided this. All he had to do was wait a minute, damn it! But no, he was too proud. He wouldn't let himself be guided, poor boy! He had already escaped them. All he had to do was wait a little and we had won. He was almost a friend already. One more sad event to deplore . . .

He sighed as he passed his hand over his face.

THEY WERE SITTING ON A LOG most likely destined for export; the owner hadn't yet put it in the water to float it downstream. He wasn't in any rush.

She was in tears and sitting on his lap. He consoled her as if she were an unhappy child. When it fell, the tree had opened a large hole in the canopy, and the moon lit their black faces brightly.

The girl's explosion of distress put him in an indefinable state of confused despair. It wasn't that he had never heard a woman cry before; he had done nothing else throughout his life. In Bamila, and this was the custom throughout the country, women dedicated at least eight full days to mourning at the death of the most pathetic runt or wasted old man. But listening to Odilia cry and mumble, he felt his courage dissolve like a lump of sugar in water. Seeing her knot her fingers together, he felt his strength abandon him little by little. He knew that as long as she cried, he couldn't make a decision. Yet it was important to act quickly; so he tried to stop her from crying. It was as if he had a little sister, the one he had dreamed of; she was profoundly distraught about something, crying, and all he could do was sit there and listen, impotent.

No, she couldn't continue to cry like this. She had to understand that she couldn't continue to cry like this. At least not right now. Later, she would have all the time in the world.

He stroked her hair and her cheeks and dried her tears with his fingers.

"Don't cry like that," he begged.

"Banda . . . Banda! My only brother! You were all I had . . . Banda, will you abandon me?" She stuttered between sobs.

When he heard that, he also felt like crying. He dreamed of Koumé . . . Such a brave boy . . . So kind, a real tough . . . They didn't make them like him anymore. He, Banda, would never get that lead, he'd never get that lead . . . Had he guessed what would happen he'd have asked him right away. Now he had left with his secret . . . He would never get that tip! So now what was he supposed to do? He couldn't just let his mother suffer like this and die broken-hearted. Sobs rose in his throat, compressing his chest. Hey! He thought, those women who go to weep at every wake, perhaps they only have to think about their own tragedies for tears to pour down their cheeks in veritable little torrents. I had always wondered how they succeeded in producing such an outflow of tears with such ease. The result was that he forgot his mother and the tip that might have allowed him to take ten thousand francs from a Greek, just ten thousand . . . just enough to provide a little happiness to his poor mother.

"Don't cry like that, little sister."

His sense of kinship grew and grew. All of a sudden he remembered what the young girl had said: "Wouldn't you like to be my brother as well?" and her candid, her innocent, air in saying it. At the time, it had amused him no end. How could he have predicted such tragic events? Now he was thinking about it again and he felt an indefinable sense of kinship and complicity binding them ever tighter.

She had calmed down. At Banda's urging, she rose to her feet.

They walked side by side under the cover of the trees. From time to time, their shadows crossed an area that was illuminated by the moon. Banda had taken her arm. They were quiet, as was the forest around them and the river on whose banks they were walking.

They arrived at the dock. Many canoes were beached on the sand or moored to a tree, a log, or a peg driven into the ground. He had her sit on a long canoe: he wanted to give her the strongest sense of security possible. But he was forced to search the surrounding gloom under the bushes that encircled the pier for a long time before finally locating a paddle. It was beautiful, large and flat at both extremities, rounded out and tapering all the way to the middle where there was a kind of knot. He congratulated himself at length on this discovery—it would make the crossing much easier. He came back and pushed with all his might to set the craft afloat. The wood ground slowly against the sand, then the canoe suddenly began to rock. He jumped in, leaning over the stern.

The boat sliced softly through the water. Banda moved the paddle mechanically in a supple and easy manner that made the water gurgle.

As far as the eye could see, upstream and down, there was only the pale river. Slow, compact masses of water pressed against each other. They spread out, turned over, stretched, and seemed to offer themselves to the grim moon that wrapped them in a cold gray mantle. The river followed a docile course between walls of vegetation. In the back of Banda's mind, the memory was slowly taking shape, climbing and getting closer, despite himself, as he continued to paddle with regular and mechanical movements. Where had he seen something more or less like this before? Where had he seen this? Yes, a missionary had died in Tanga; a very old and venerated Catholic missionary. The long quietly tame river under the sickly moonlight reminded him of the procession that followed the body of that old missionary. The vast crowd had calmly arranged itself in rows behind the hearse and followed it through the streets. Yes, at this particular moment, this is what he recalled as he looked at the sad ritual of this river he knew so well: a monochrome spectacle, a dream sequence, a nightmare. Yes, that night, after such a sad day, this river gave him the ineluctable sensation of a nightmare.

The water lapped the hull. Banda looked at the young girl slumped in the bow. From time to time Odilia's chest expanded suddenly, and her sorrow would escape in little uneven gasps.

"Odilia!" Banda would implore in a reproachful voice. But the young girl would then moan pathetically, irresistibly; her voice would ascend little by little until it exploded into the night like the cry of a mortally wounded animal. No, he wouldn't scold her for crying anymore. Yeah! He shouldn't blame her for crying; besides, it only made her cry harder. She wasn't doing it on purpose; it was out of her control. He would stroke her hair and cheek when they were back on land. Yes, that's it—he would simply stroke her hair and cheek when they were walking side by side. Perhaps then she would be quiet. He couldn't stand to hear her sobs.

The canoe came aground, grinding against the sand. He noticed that the bump had propelled him far from the stern where he was perched. Hah! I constantly let my mind wander and never think about what I am doing, he admonished himself. He took a quick look behind him. And to think that he had just crossed the river without even looking out for what he was doing, and with the river this high the current could have caused him to drift. Would he ever lose this bad habit of thinking of something besides what he was doing? He took the young girl in his arms and set her little naked feet down in the dry sand.

While they walked along this wide path that Banda knew so well he regularly stroked her hair. She wasn't crying anymore; rather, she relieved her tension by exhaling loudly and violently, like a muffled explosion. Nobody crossed their path, and Banda was happy about it.

The young man wet his lips.

"You see, little sister," he began, "whatever the reason, whenever they want to catch someone and they can't, they take it out on his parents back home, or his wife, or his brothers . . . I'm sure that they'll hassle your parents . . . Perhaps they'll wrap a rope around their necks and drag them back to Tanga so they can torture and interrogate them every day. They may hold them in their prison for months and months and, who knows, perhaps even years. We have to try to prevent that. If your brother were alive, his life would be worth having your parents suffer a bit, right? But now . . . You understand what I'm trying to say. Now, there's no reason for them to bother your parents. You can't mistreat the living for something you hold against the dead. No, nobody can do that. Not even them . . ."

He was speaking to her in a hushed voice, as you might use with an unhappy child; it was a voice that was all compassion. He was speaking to her with every possible care being careful not to mention Koumé's name, to not speak of the young man's death—things that made her cry.

"That's why we have to show them that your brother is no longer of this world, that there's no reason to bother the living. I am leading you to my mother's where you'll sleep. If, after I leave, she asks you questions, tell her that you're my girlfriend. Tell her without being modest and also tell her that you have violent headaches. But above all, please little sister, don't cry too much: my poor mother is ill. I'm going back. I'll take the body down the river in the canoe and leave it out in the open under the Tanga bridge."

He took a long pause and examined the young girl to see if she was reacting at all. He couldn't make out her expression—only that a vast sorrow was taking its toll.

"You and I, we know nothing," he resumed. "After your brother's escape, you took refuge with me, your boyfriend, because you'd taken fright: that's what you tell them if they come this way. You never know. Do you promise to do that?"

She nodded yes.

I should have had a little sister like that. Yeah! She certainly loved her brother. She sure loved him. Are there many sisters out there who love their brothers that much? I should have had a little sister just like that . . . Would she finally have wound up getting married, leaving, abandoning me? Odilia sure loved her brother.

Still, his mother had loved him, and still did, unwaveringly. He also loved his mother right now, with all his might. To tell the truth, he had always felt that the bond between them was exceptional, and could only be explained by unusual circumstances: for example, the early death of his father that left them alone in the world, and those agonizing moments of separation when he was a schoolboy in Tanga. These were the things that explained why they loved each other so much. No, people like them couldn't be common. Still, if he'd always dreamed of a loving little sister, it was mostly because he craved tenderness—though he wasn't entirely aware of this. He wanted a tenderness that would warm him when his mother died.

And last night, he had realized that other men loved each other with an intensity that he would never have guessed. Love, as a human sentiment, took him by surprise, left him breathless.

He had always wanted a little sister, but without ever trying to understand why. Now he knew . . . A little sister just like that, loving, courageous, and the rest. The path led out into the open.

They came to the red dirt road.

"My place is close by."

Indeed, beyond the next bend lay Bamila, two endless rows of huts lining the road. The town was slumbering lazily in the heart of the forest, lining this road born in Tanga. Bamila the ferocious was relaxed and sleeping. The front yards, consisting of two long strips running parallel with the road, were filled with small livestock, snoring pigs, ruminating sheep; here and there you could make out a timorous little short-haired dog curled up in a ball, or the furtive shadow of a cat stalking fresh blood. The huts were silent and dark.

Hey! Banda said gathering himself up, someone's in my mother's place . . . A man's voice! That's odd at this hour. Who could it be? What could he be saying to her? Who could be there at such an hour?

It must have been late . . . Was it really all that late? Maybe it wasn't. A chimpanzee began to howl in the distance as if to answer his question. No, it wasn't that late. It was certainly possible that someone might come speak with his mother then. In fact, if he had lived in the house alone, nobody would come to visit, with the exception of the dedicated women friends such as Sabina, Regina, and the others who came to nurse his mother. For her part, she seemed to enjoy people coming to see her to discuss endless nonsense. So who could it be? Tonga! Yes, that was his voice all right; he could recognize it. Tonga! He was one of the men of Bamila who hated him most, something Banda returned in kind. Tonga seemed an inoffensive old man except that he was boastful, a liar and a hypocrite, and could hold a pretty good grudge.

Banda pushed the door open. Tonga recognized him instantly and cried out:

"Well! Is that you Banda? It turns out your mother was getting anxious. Well, who have you brought with you?"

"Do I ask what you had to eat today?" Banda answered sharply as he took tentative steps toward his mother, still holding Odilia by the hand.

Tonga wore a wrap covering his legs to his belt: his stomach and chest were naked despite the cool night. Indeed, what really characterized the man was a complete lack of concern for the surrounding temperature and an almost unflappably good health accented by a muscular strength rarely seen at such an age. He stood next to the door.

The young man's answer apparently hadn't impressed him much: he looked used to this kind of exchange.

The son was standing in front of his mother. She was an emaciated, curled-up thing moving spasmodically like a black crayfish on the bamboo cot grown shiny from use. He watched for her reaction. The logs burned with a small flickering flame; on the walls, the shadows danced, both mocking and scary.

Again, Tonga's insidious voice asserted itself.

"Sabina told us what happened, told us everything . . ."

"By the way," Banda worried, though calm now, "what are you doing here at this hour?"

"So, is he now going to prevent my visiting a sick woman? Where did you ever hear that one wasn't to visit a sick

woman? Ah! These children . . . They don't have enough
with fighting and struggling! They have to fight against a
custom as old as looking in on a sick woman."

Tonga finished his sentence with a little sardonic laugh.
Banda had to bite his lip to keep from exploding. Only one
person is saving you, and that's my mother! he thought.
Oh! Without her I would have already kicked you out of the
house and you'd be the worse for wear.

Yes, his mother knew. The women had told her everything. Had she cried a lot? And what was he to say to her
now? He didn't know what he was going to tell her. He sat
down on the bed at the other side of the fire, holding Odilia
close; the warmth of the room seemed to revive her.

The patient, visibly intrigued, was looking at them both.
Her eyes shone with a strange light. It looked as if all remaining life had lodged there. Faced with this piercing gaze,
Banda felt as if he had just committed some grave sin, even
though he couldn't think of what it might be. The strength
radiating from that look froze him on the spot and left him
breathless. Yes, she had suffered greatly. She was probably
surprised, overjoyed to see them.

He moistened his lips:

"Mother," Banda mumbled, "perhaps you expect me to
say something? They put my cacao on the fire. My uncle
says they just pretended. But I saw them put my cacao on
the fire. They said it was bad. Mother, they really said that.
But it's not true. My cacao wasn't bad. I know that's false. I
swear that I followed all their recommendations. I did nothing but follow their recommendations. The problem is those
people have no compassion."

He stopped talking; he was out of breath. They were all
silent. The eyes of the sick woman now fixed the dancing
flame. Her absent air was more painful to Banda than anything.

"I wanted to get married, to make you happy just once
before you die," he went on. "The problem is I can't anymore. My father's dead, and to those who can hear me, I
swear that it's not my fault: I did what I could. I can no

longer get married before you die: where would I find the money?"

While he was speaking, he observed his mother: she was oddly silent. She looked more absent than ever. Was she suffering horribly? How could he know? One can usually recognize the pain caused by a wound, an abscess, something visible. But who can assess the pain lodged at the bottom of someone's heart?

Suddenly, he realized that he had forgotten Odilia. Ah, yes! He was still holding her hand . . . He quickly squeezed it to tell her that he wasn't forgetting her, that he couldn't forget her. Then his thoughts returned to his mother. He had to console her, get that over with. He had another task to accomplish, a very important one: he had to save another mother from useless and odious brutality. Perhaps it wasn't too late? He might have time; he would if he hurried. And assuming nothing had happened to the body . . . No, certainly, nothing had happened. What could happen? Nobody took that path. Who would? He started; he had to be careful not to be seen with the corpse. Someone might accuse him of having killed Koumé. At this idea horrible thoughts flitted through his mind.

He would be careful not to be caught with the body. My God! This was all so complicated! His mother, Tonga, Koumé, Odilia, the cacao, the marriage, was this what life was all about? Did life have nothing but this on tap for him?

"Mother, perhaps you heard that they beat me and gave me a black eye. But it's nothing, Mother, it's really nothing; it doesn't even hurt anymore. They also took me to the police station. That wasn't a big deal either. A White man released me, a White officer."

Banda noticed the glow of admiration that crept furtively across his mother's face; haggard and motionless, she remained expressionless.

"I beg you, Mother, don't worry too much about me. I'll be fine without a wife. I'll prepare my own meals. It's not exactly unheard of . . . Besides, it's not my fault . . . In any case, I'll get by, don't you worry. I'll remember you. I'll never forget you. I did my best, but I failed. I worked all year for nothing. If only I could have known that beforehand. Mother, there are people, like me, for example, who have no luck. I assure you, neither of us can do anything about it."

He said any old thing that went through his head. All of a sudden, life was proving to be very complicated, extremely complicated, more than he'd ever experienced. Tonga was now also getting involved. What was he saying? As he tried to listen, he felt waves of weariness flow over him, as if he were trying to accomplish something that he knew was useless. Odilia's hand had remained in his own and he squeezed it several times. No, he wasn't forgetting her. A kind of complicity, a secret, bound them together. For how long? And what about this inexplicable sense of kinship? Had she really felt it? Perhaps she'd said that earlier just to win him over to her cause, to trick him.

Despite his lassitude, he heard:

"You see, son. Every time something bad happens, first check that it isn't your own fault. We hold in ourselves the source of all the bad that happens to us. Banda, I am your father. How many times have I warned you? I said, 'Son, you behave like a madman. The light of day and the vastness of the universe dazzle you. You don't pay close enough attention. Who ever lived such a carefree life, oblivious to what surrounds him?' Have you listened to me? Have you given up your drinking, your fighting? Have you given up sleeping with other men's women? You know I warned you that you wouldn't get away with these things forever . . . God had pity on me, and my words haven't gone to waste: he struck you."

The old man was triumphant: that explained why he was here at this hour. He was triumphant and wanted to savor the spectacle of Banda's misery. Banda wasn't impressed and wanted to egg him on.

"My word! You actually believe in God?"

"What kind of a question is that?" Tonga shot back, without giving up the sardonic laugh so much a part of him it seemed a reflex.

"It's just hard to tell," Banda answered.

The other took this as an opportunity to argue. You could tell he wasn't afraid to talk tonight.

"I'm not baptized? How important is that? Tell me? And our ancestors who believed in God, what kind of baptism did they receive, I ask you? Still, they believed in God, son. No, being baptized is unimportant . . . God simply observed our relative roles as father and son. He came down on my side because, whether baptized or not, a father is a father . . ."

"Even if he isn't righteous?"

"I've always been straight with you, son."

It was Banda's turn to let out a little sardonic laugh. He had this foul old man at his mercy, or he was about to.

"No! Who are you trying to fool that you've always been straight with me? That's not true—you've never been straight! I asked you to help me by talking to my fiancée's father. Why did you refuse? You're old: he might have listened to you. He would have looked on me more kindly: in any case, he would have asked for less. Huh? Speak! Why did you refuse? I'm the one asking now."

Tonga had stopped showing off. Perhaps he hadn't expected this question. He had imagined that Banda's bad luck had broken him and that the young man would let him triumph. He was quiet and you could imagine him in the shadows on the other side of the room, thinking. Banda thought he was cornered and wanted to finish him off.

"Speak, Tonga, I'm listening. Why did you refuse to do me a favor that cost you nothing, you who have always been straight with me?"

"You've mocked me too many times," the old man said, almost reluctantly.

"I've mocked you too many times? What does that mean, I've mocked you too many times? Is it that I stood up to you in our conversations? I only ask you this: who married Zombi? You, right? You, his father . . . Who in Bamila doesn't know that at the time your son Zombi was constantly doing you wrong? Didn't he even come close to hitting you one day? Yet, when it came time to getting him married, you forgave everything and you did what it took. When it comes to me, you can't even forgive the smallest offense. No, you aren't a father to me, and how could I consider myself to be your son? No, Tonga, my father, my real father, is in the other world, alas. If he were still alive, I would be married today. I would have as many wives as I wanted. You may be his brother, but let me tell you, it's still not enough for you to be my father . . ."

He stopped suddenly. Would he argue with this old man the rest of his life? In all the time that had passed since this had started, what had it gotten him?

"Banda," Tonga cried out suddenly, with a broken voice that caused the young man to jump, "Banda, you are mistaken! You are wrong! I swear to you that I never wanted to harm you. My dead ancestors are my witness. I only wanted what was best for you! I swear to you son, I only wanted the best . . ."

"If only I could know what that was . . ."

"Well, that's precisely the point, son, that's it precisely! You said it yourself. You don't know what's best for you and what isn't. I'll bet you don't know. Say, let's not speak of me anymore, ok? Don't you know that all of Bamila hates you? And why is that? Can a whole village hate you for no reason? Think about it, son. It can't be for no reason."

He was silent, as if to measure the effect of his argument on his antagonist. Perhaps, in his mind, this last point had such strength that it would cause the young man if not to capitulate, at least to adjust his attitude. And then he went on:

"This is what we old people say, and only this: 'Don't leave the path of your fathers to follow in the White people's tracks: they are only out to fool you.' All a White person has ever wanted is to make tons of money. And when he has his fortune, he abandons you and takes the boat back to his country, to his own folks . . . While he was causing you to forget, or at least to look down on your family, he hasn't forgotten his for an instant. A White man has no friends and only lies: he goes back to his country and tells everyone that we are cannibals. Do you see me, or your grandfather, or your great grandfather, all those whom I mention so often, eating human flesh? Yuck! Don't allow yourself to be drawn in by the Whites. What do they bring you? Nothing. What do they leave you? Nothing. Not even a little money. Only disdain for your own people, for those who gave you life . . ."

Banda was terrified. A cold shiver ran up and down his spine. His eyes rested on Odilia. The young girl, fascinated, looked at the old man who was speaking from the darkened corner. Her eyes were wide open: she probably couldn't see him very well.

Banda couldn't get over his surprise. After what had happened to him today, he had to agree that old Tonga was at least partly right. It's true that the White man's only friend is money. White men only want the most money possible. Even when the missionaries speak of God, all they are really trying to do is to get you to contribute to the collection plate. Yeah! That's true, when a White man wants to make money, you'd better not get in his way—otherwise you'll get what happened to Koumé. Poor boy! Poor Odilia's brother!

"No, I swear to you son, I never wanted to hurt you. All I wanted was what was best for you. But you and I can't understand each other. You and I can't: it's as if we were speaking different languages."

His tone of sincerity surprised Banda. Perhaps he's right; perhaps he only wanted the best for me.

He felt as if he and Tonga were in two different canoes on an immense rushing river. They were reaching out to each other. Their hands touched and, intertwining, clung together. They began to pull at each other, each trying to force the other into his own boat, to have the other person join him. But they each kept on pulling. The rapid water caused the canoes to drift apart and with every passing minute the distance got greater. Finally, tired of the battle, they let go, and each one drifted off in his respective direction, full of spite for the other.

Damn! Perhaps he's right. But then he was even more suspicious. Why had he never spoken to him like this before? And why was he talking about White people today? What did Whites have to do with his and Tonga's dislike for each other? Oh, yeah, Whites are his hobbyhorse. Just as quickly Banda reassured himself, maybe the old man had felt backed into a corner and had chosen this escape route? Whites are his obsession. All of a sudden he decided not to think about it. It certainly wasn't worth it.

"Mother," he said, "this is my girlfriend. She's very sick. Let her sleep. Don't speak with her too much."

"Always these girlfriends!" Tonga commented, between clenched teeth, and as if speaking to himself. "Is that a way to live? And your women, your real wives, when will we see them?"

"Say, Tonga, are you really that worried about it?"

"What do I have to do with it? Old folks don't even have the right to comment anymore. What do I have to do with it? But our own fathers didn't raise us this badly. If you like a girl, you go find her father and you give him what he wants. From that point on that woman will be yours. But you, you take the first woman you see: you live with her, under the same roof, for days, weeks, months, years. Then, one day, just like that, you leave her or she leaves you. Is that a way to live your life, son, tell me the truth? That's White folks' behavior . . ."

The old man looked fixedly at the ground, as if immersed in some grim meditation. But the young man, who had now risen to his feet, had already stopped listening to him. He was looking at the sick woman.

"Mother, I have to leave. Don't ask me where I'm going. Only know this: I have to leave at all cost. I'll be back tomorrow morning."

She remained silent. Was she already communicating with the dead? He'd always thought about when she would get revenge against all those who had already traveled to what she called the land beyond the river. What would I say to them? she had always asked herself fearfully. Perhaps she was already preparing her defense. She must feel closer to death than ever.

In recent days, it had seemed that the prospect of witnessing her son's wedding was keeping her alive. This idea was the hope around which she had rebuilt her life after that long-ago event that was her husband's death. Now that she had lost all hope, nothing connected her to a life that she must consider absurd, that she surely wanted to exit as soon as possible.

In leaving, Banda closed the door behind him. As he walked away, he could hear Tonga moan:

"How I feel sorry for children today. What does life have in store for these dimwits! Always doing whatever they want, is that a way to live? At their age, we didn't even think of ourselves as men. We even went naked or close to it. And our parent's presence was daunting! It intimidated us. But kids today, that's another story! Because they're dressed in fine clothes, they shamelessly show off their girlfriends in front of our astonished eyes! They don't even spare us. What's this world coming to?"

As he ran like a demon, he was thinking of Tonga. He couldn't understand this old man or those like him—and there were many of them in Bamila. Tonga claimed he was old and experienced. But what does he take me for? An idiot who understands nothing?

Yeah! He almost got me with his fine words: "No, I swear to you son, I never wanted to hurt you. I only wanted what was best for you . . . I'll bet you don't know what's best for you and what isn't." Try that on someone else! To think I almost fell for it. Does he think I remember nothing? Rotten old bastard!

Say! Once I fought with his son—and he started it—he didn't want to pay back a loan! That little runt almost died. Tonga snuck off to consult with the local mirror-man. When he returned he said that if Zombi was in pain, it wasn't from fighting. After all, wasn't his son strong enough to teach me a lesson? No, if he was in such bad shape, it was because I had relied on magic to cross Zombi. Because I was jealous of him because I don't have a wife. He claimed that the mirror-man had said that. Because my mother asked me to, I had to take my turn before the mirror-man, who formally denied all of Tonga's claims. Bah! Bah! Old bastard! And to say he almost got me back there. And I didn't mean you any ill . . . And we don't understand each other anymore . . . And it's as if we spoke different languages . . . And can a whole village like Bamila hate you for no reason? Old bastard!

If Banda held such a grudge against old Tonga, it wasn't
because he had slandered him—he didn't care about slan-
der; it was far more about having forced him to go before
the mirror-man, about whom he had always expressed a
haughty indifference. He could not forgive the old man
for having forced him into such an obvious about-face. He
couldn't remember the scene without disgust: the naked
sorcerer in front of his mirror, vain and pretentious, with
his gesticulating and incantations, and that whole useless
and pitiable ritual. How could anybody give any credence
to that ranting? Still, he had been forced to exculpate himself in this way. His mother stressed that if he refused, he
would be proving Tonga's gross accusations to the people of
Bamila.

Another time he covered me in curses. He had asked me
to go cut down trees in his field; all the while, his son had
been off God knows where on a weeklong bender. I refused,
of course. Hey . . . I'm not that stupid. Yeah: he marries off
his son and I have to sweat blood to feed him, his daughter-
in-law, and his idiot son . . . No, I'm not that dumb. Oh,
what the hell! What's the point of thinking of all this now?
If I had to remember all the things he's done to me I'd never
be through with it. And he claims to be a father to me. They
all claim it because they are my father's brothers or half-
brothers. But that's not enough. They should understand
that that's not enough, they really need to understand that
. . . But they are so unused to people like me. I'll bet they've
never seen someone who defends himself the way I do. Not
a single one of them actually wants what's best for me. What
they really want is that I should play the fool for them, like
the others. I should behave like a son who is docile, obedient, respectful, and helpful, and all the rest but . . . with
nothing in exchange! Yeah, right! Oh, at least I got something out of going to school: I learned not to be duped by
old men. I know that not a single one of them is looking out
for my interests. They don't like people who stir things up,
especially if those people don't act exactly as they do. They
want everyone to sleep when they sleep, cry when they cry,

laugh with them, stay at home when they aren't going out, and follow them in generating empty talk and badmouthing others. You want to leave, if only to Tanga? You have to ask their permission, and their blessing and then listen without flinching to their endless, useless, and stupid advice. If you have just wed a woman, you'd think they'd want you to undress her in front of them so they could inspect her in every detail! A son who is docile, obedient, respectful . . . helpful and all. That's what they want.

Even though she's sick, I'm surprised my mother continues to deal with these snakes. "Pity, pity for my son!" she moans. She is absolutely convinced that these braggarts could throw a spell on me, though I've always wondered how they would accomplish that. It's true that they always imply, insidiously, that they have supernatural powers. Some people actually believe them. Idiots. Damn! My mother believes it, and she's a Christian. And the missionaries hate nothing more than those types of stories. If the priests in Tanga knew that my mother had forced me to go to the mirror-man, they would have refused her the sacrament for a long time, a very long time. Hey! That's the only point where my mother and the missionaries disagree. My mother says that if Satan really exists, as the preachers claim, then why would such a power be refused to men such as Tonga or the healer?

For my part, I don't have time to think of all that nonsense. What really disgusts me is that other young people, including orphans, have so little courage; that they can go ahead and let themselves be walked all over by those folks, by Tonga and the rest. They would never dare speak face to face with an old man. One doesn't confront an old man, even if he isn't your father, and especially not if he is. Isn't an old man, a father, an uncle, or whatever, just a human being, though? Ah! If only one could explain that to young folks. It's impossible to explain to them that you can confront anyone who isn't treating you fairly. In fact, with a few exceptions they also hate me; they just don't dare say it out loud.

My God! I won't stay another week in Bamila after my
mother dies. Damn! I don't want her to die. I love her too
much to want her dead. But what if she were to die soon?
Well, in that case—I would go to Fort-Nègre. Yeah! But Tonga was right about the Whites. Even the missionaries with
their robes, their crosses, and their long beards—they are
wilier . . . And a hundred francs if you want to go to confession, and two hundred francs if you want to baptize your
kid . . . And a thousand francs if you want to get married in
front of a priest . . . And five hundred for the tithe . . . And
the same for them to accept your son in their school . . .
And so much for the Catholic mission bells to toll at your
mother's death! For all of them, it's about money. Only, a
missionary is wilier. "I'm in agony now, Father. I've been
waiting for you. Approach, I beg of you, and hear my sins
. . ." "Just a minute, son, have you paid your tithe for this
year?"

Hey! Oh! Yeah, that's it—I've got it! Yes, now I understand what it is. White folks and old men are essentially the
same—exactly the same . . . Damn! Is that really true? Old
men and White folks are the same? No! It's not. A White
man isn't exactly like an elder. A White man is about money, lots of money, and always more money . . . A White
man wants to make money and that's all. An old man is a
lot more complicated. You have to listen to him all day and
all night. You always have to approve of what he is saying,
admire it. You have to say he's right, that he's wise, that
he's seen the entire world, that he knows many things, even
when he's clearly a doddering idiot. No, that's not true: a
White man is not exactly like an old man. For example,
an elder from Bamila won't ever want to exploit you for
money. He attaches almost no importance to money. He'd
even give some to you if he had any. Yes, he'd give you some
as long as you admire him, as long as you extol his wisdom,
his insight. He may, on occasion, say: "Son, come help me
with my field, please. You see, I'm getting old, I no longer
have the strength . . ." But that's legitimate, especially if he's
got no sons—Tonga, for his part, has a son. And in fact, that

rarely happens. Whereas a White man just wants to make money and then go back to his country. And beware of the whip should you refuse to work.

What's better? A White man from Tanga or an old man from Bamila? . . . Damn! What's better! If only someone could tell him . . . What's better. He passed his hand over his forehead without being able to answer his own question. And then, instead of opposing an old man from Bamila with a White man from Tanga, he now compared Bamila and Tanga. What was better, Tanga or Bamila? . . . Bamila or Tanga? . . . Bamila or Fort-Nègre? He had lived in Tanga, which he knew well; he could only imagine Fort-Nègre in the image of Tanga, except more beautiful. What was better: Bamila or Tanga? Bamila or Fort-Nègre?

In response to this question, he thought of all of the generous and devoted women who had repeatedly helped him, who took turns nursing his mother at her sickbed, keeping her company, consoling her, making her life just a little more bearable. These same women had helped him carry the cacao—was it their fault if the inspectors had thrown it on the fire? Sabina, Regina . . . As his mind wandered toward these women he couldn't keep from thinking of them. In Tanga, there was nobody like these women—and so much the less in Fort-Nègre? And to think that they took care of his mother all day, every day, without fail, without complaining. Sabina . . . Regina . . ." Have you forgotten that all of Bamila hates you?" That's not true. Old bastard! Not all of Bamila hated him; that wasn't true. And those women, Sabina . . . Regina . . . And so many others, did they hate him? On the contrary, they loved him like a son. Hadn't they done everything possible to snatch him back from the clutches of the regional guards? It's true that, to the pity, the commiseration, the compassion and care of the people of Bamila, he preferred the total indifference, the cruelty of the inhabitants of North Tanga, who—just like the White people—were too preoccupied with their own affairs. It was only because of his mother that he felt anything for Bamila.

If what had happened to Koumé had taken place in Bamila, even if they hadn't liked him that much beforehand, as long as he lived there, the whole village would certainly have sided with him. It had happened many times. In Tanga, the event instead went almost unnoticed.

Those women, Sabina, Regina, they never stopped taking care of his mother. In Tanga, who would have taken care of her like that? He was bent on leaving Bamila after her death, but he could already tell that because of those women he would always feel nostalgia for his native village. He was still running, or almost. He looked carefully around him, examined the path, trying to situate himself between the river and the main road. Hey! He had just completed more than half the route without even realizing it. His habit of thinking about something besides what he was doing . . .

The moon had disappeared; the darkness was intense. The sky was speckled with twinkling stars; at least it wasn't raining.

It was a good thing the moon had set; someone crossing his path might have recognized him.

Chimpanzees howled in the distance accompanied by a thumping that sounded like a drum. My God! How do they make that strange noise? he thought. Who will tell me how they do it? Some say that they strike their fists against the base of large trees. But the base of even a large tree is always more or less at the level of the ground; and everyone knows that at night, chimpanzees sleep in the treetops. Would a chimpanzee ever come down out of the treetop where he is resting just to beat at the base of the tree? How do they make this noise? Perhaps by beating their chests as others say? But that would mean having an incredibly strong thorax, one that is very resonant . . . The chimpanzees kept howling while accompanying themselves with the same panting and dull drum-like thud: he understood that it was only four or five hours from daybreak. He would have to hurry if he didn't want to be seen with the body . . .

He carried a change of clothes under his arm: the others were too dirty; he wouldn't be able to show himself in public without attracting attention. He would change when he was done. Yeah! Let's hope nothing had happened to the body. What an idea! Could anything happen to it? He suddenly thought of Odilia and he again felt this strange sense of kinship and connection. He was still running, or almost. He was sweating! While thinking of Odilia he felt as if travelling through a pocket of warm air, and for a moment his heart sped up.

He came out onto the river; the still darkness floated over it. He jumped into the long canoe that he had used earlier and left the bank with quick paddle-strokes.

He hoped nothing had happened to the body. But what could possibly happen to it? Why did he, Banda, never have any luck? He had sworn to save a man's life no matter what, and yet that man had died faster than if he had promised nothing. Perhaps he shouldn't have sworn to save him? Something or someone seemed to be bent on undoing all his best-laid plans. If they knew about this in Bamila, what would the old men say? "Are you unaware that all Bamila hates you? Can a whole village like Bamila hate you without there being a reason for it?" What does all Bamila mean, anyway? Twenty or thirty old men . . . And what does he make of all the rest? Of women like Sabina, Regina . . . and there are hundreds of them! What does he make of them? What, I ask you? It's true that he and I speak different languages.

And what would the old men say if they had known about all this in Bamila? That he's cursed; that he'd always be a good-for-nothing . . . If only he had been able to sell his cacao, he would have married; that way he would have proved to his uncle, to the old men, that one can behave like this and still succeed. But is that really true? Could one really behave as he does and succeed?

And to think that all it would have taken was a word from the controller. For example, he could have said, "Nice cacao . . ." and that would have been quite enough. He, Banda, would have gone to find Mr. Pallogakis, and he would have asked him (in French): "How much would you pay

me per kilo? Sixty francs? . . . That's fine!" And while Mr.
Pallogakis was calculating the total, he would do the same,
just to show Mr. Pallogakis that he wasn't a fool and that he
shouldn't try to swindle him. He would have controlled the
whole weighing operation himself and checked the result.
That Mr. Pallogakis surely had some odd ways of manipu-
lating the scale. My God! What was he thinking of now?

No, it wasn't his fault if Koumé was dead. That boy was
simply too proud; he couldn't let himself be guided. He had
wanted to take the walkway on his own, without a sound,
just so he could say that nobody had guided him. Poor boy!
A tough one, Odilia's brother was a tough one, a real tough
one . . . But whose fault was it if he was dead? Banda nevertheless felt a nagging sense of guilt.

The canoe scraped against the sand. He took advantage
of his own forward momentum to leap out the front of the
boat. He would never get over the habit of thinking about
one thing while doing another—he would never get over
that habit, it was in his blood. He was running along the
bank in the direction of the body. Suddenly, he stopped. No,
this wasn't the right thing to do. He retraced his steps, got
back into the canoe, and set it afloat again by planting the
paddle into the sand and pushing off hard. He went down
the river closely following the right bank. He was alone in
the dark night; that kept indiscreet eyes off him. He felt
a comforting sense of complicity despite his solitude; he
wanted the assistance of no one but the night.

The heavy, turbulent water of the stream lapped up
against the wooden gunwale; the boat rocked dangerously;
he tied it off downstream and came back up the path.

Here is where, earlier, he had told Koumé, "Wait . . .
Watch out . . . I'll strike a match . . ." If he had only waited,
he wouldn't be dead now. He was hungry; he thought bitterly that it would be a long while before he got to eat. He
should not have forgotten to eat in Bamila. He was completely sober now. Hey! On this side of the stream, the bank
wasn't raised; it was so only on the other side where he had

fought to save Odilia. From here it was easy to get into the streambed.

He walked on the cold stone, causing water to splash up at every step, his face straining forward. Let's hope nobody had found the body . . . Let's hope nobody had found it. Who could find it? . . . He touched the rigid and icy body that had been so alive only a while ago. He turned it over, felt it, and inspected it, as much as he was able in the dark. No, nothing had happened to it.

Still, he wasn't a bad guy, he thought, without realizing that in doing so he was taking on the prejudices of the old pagan Tonga and of his Christian mother for whom one's morality in life predetermined the kind of death one would have. Instinctively he looked for Koumé's eyes, but his gaze finally didn't dare find them; as if he could see him despite the darkness, as if he feared the expression death might have affixed to the dead man's face, perhaps a horrible grimace, an atrocious scowl. He had seen many cases of violent death: road accidents had provided an almost daily sample. But a man whose head was bashed in as he drowned, that he had never seen.

He was afraid of seeing on this face how badly Odilia's brother had suffered. Perhaps he hadn't suffered at all? Or perhaps he had suffered beyond what was imaginable? Had he died as soon as his head struck the rock? Or had the water completed the rock's work by entering his mouth, his nostrils, and so forth, slowly freezing his blood with its icy contact?

He stretched the body out in the canoe, took up his place in the stern. He paddled softly, just enough to gain momentum. Then it was just a matter of steering the long craft that the strong current, magnified by the recent flooding, carried along. It was nevertheless not an easy task. Banda hadn't navigated this stretch in a very long time. If he stayed in the middle of the river there was the risk of flipping, because the current was always very powerful at that point. Nor could he move along the banks; all sorts of sunken obstacles were strewn along the edge where the water was almost stagnant. He thought he had resolved the problem by remaining halfway between the bank and the middle. The only remaining problem was the reefs. How could he avoid the reefs? He knew that this section of the river was riddled with rocks. But how was he supposed to spot them through the screen of darkness?

He was sitting in the stern of the canoe, tense, focused. At each instant he expected the worst, and he was already shaking. Damn! How to avoid the reefs? What if the water level had risen to the point where they were submerged? And perhaps he would pass over without even touching them? Yes and no, he countered himself, it's not possible. Some may have disappeared under the water, but others will be right at the surface, I know it. There are also shoals; those, the water can't entirely cover up; water has never covered them entirely. How can one avoid those? A reef was surely going to pierce the hull . . . And he wouldn't be able to continue. It was sure to happen; it had to happen. Somebody had it out for him; someone took pleasure in undermining all of his plans, especially, the best laid, the ones that meant the most to him.

The canoe slid softly, silently, over the water. Banda felt as if he were committing adultery by blending in this way with the silence, with the night, with the solitude. He felt a kind of intoxication: what he was experiencing took over and kept him from thinking about his misery, his other reality. Only this reality counted right now: it was exclusive; that's why it made him feel drunk.

He was tense, wound up. At every moment he felt as if the canoe were impaling itself on a rocky outcropping. But nothing was happening, which, paradoxically, created a kind of disappointment. He looked into the night, his face tense, his eyes narrowed. He had traveled half the distance that had separated him from Tanga, from the reinforced concrete bridge.

He was starting to gain confidence, to breathe more freely, to relax . . . And that's when the accident took place.

The hull of the canoe crashed into something hard. Banda was thrown into the water and he couldn't help drinking a few mouthfuls. As quick as lightning, he regained his senses, saw the canoe between two blinks, reached his hand out haphazardly, touched the craft and held on tight. He passed the palm of his left hand that was free over his face and rubbed his eyes. The canoe was rocking heavily. Under the pressure of Banda's hand, it slowly stabilized. That's when he realized that the hull was intact. It was continuing to drift downstream; it was pursuing its course, taking Banda with it. He easily climbed back into the canoe; he hadn't let go of the paddle. How had he done that? His right hand—the same hand that reached out for the canoe—was also holding the paddle.

Lifting the body, he felt the wood at the place of impact: no water was seeping in. No damage, luckily! A reef—he had hit a reef! It had to happen, he had expected it, he had been wrong to hope otherwise. He wondered how he would fare in the next strike. Luckily, it never happened.

He made out the distant beams of a hurricane lamp and was delighted. The night-watchman at the Benedetti sawmill! Only a few kilometers separated him from the bridge now. The current was carrying him along quickly.

He stretched and exhaled. He could feel the sweat on his cheeks and forehead. He approached the bank and tried to make out a bush that would make an appropriate landing spot . . . Hey! What was happening! Damn! The canoe was spinning and rocking in place. He was going to flip over! He should have guessed—the whirlpool! Yes, that's what it was, the famous whirlpool! He should have remembered. He knew about it . . . Maybe, but the darkness would have prevented him from locating the damned thing. Someone was trying to keep him from succeeding! Someone had it out for him . . . The terror of Bamila dug his paddle furiously in the water, with all of his might, displacing tons of water in a few seconds. The canoe stopped turning . . . and rocking! Then slowly, very slowly, hesitatingly, it began to slide again . . . slowly, very slowly . . . pushed by a succession of paddle-strokes, every one as vigorous and desperate as the next. Yeah! He had just made it, that's for sure.

With the back of his hand he mopped his forehead where water and sweat were beading. He should have remembered: you don't go through the whirlpool. What had just happened to him was deadly! Luckily, he had escaped. Damn! How had he succeeded in escaping? Was he actually luckier than he thought?

Only much farther downstream did he find the bushy outcropping he sought. He powered the boat onto the bank. He lifted the body, slid it into the water, and followed it. He swam toward the bridge, slowly, silently, cautiously, looking carefully all about him. He was dragging along poor Koumé's body. At least he'll have been swimming once in his life, he thought. The solitude, the night, and the silence were starting to get to him: he told himself he would soon be finished with such allies.

Reaching a point a few meters from the bridge, he approached the bank, gained his footing, and began walking in the water while continuing to pull the body; he placed it on the sand, its feet in the water and the rest on dry land. As for himself, he never came up onto the bank; he was afraid of leaving footprints.

He was getting ready to leave Koumé, not without casting a last compassionate glance at him. At that moment, another idea came to him, another big idea! Damn! His eyes went dark with surprise. He hadn't thought about it . . . He might have left without even thinking of it! He would never have forgiven himself if he had. He tremulously reached his large hand into Koumé's right pocket after turning him on his side. He leaned over the body, working his fingers into the corners of the wet pocket. All of a sudden his fingers encountered cold steel, nothing else. He took out the little jackknife, a small object of the most common sort except that it had a corkscrew. He turned it over in his hand. No, he wouldn't take it. The police might be surprised to not find anything in Koumé's pockets . . . One never knows with those people: one has to be careful. He was still leaning

over the body. He put the knife back. He turned the body
to the other side and put his hand into Koumé's left pocket.
He was short of breath . . . His fingers felt a humid object.
He pulled out a little packet that his fumbling fingers tried
to undo; it was pieces of paper, many pieces of paper rolled
into a square of cloth. He looked more closely at the pieces
of paper . . . What could they be? He stood up and looked
more closely widening his eyes. Yeah!!! He almost fainted.
For a moment, everything began to spin. Bills! Lots and lots
of bills! Big, uncirculated, stiff, crinkly, almost dry bills. Not
little bills, but big ones, like the ones you spot only in the
hands of the Greeks . . .

He rushed back into the water. He swam with one hand
while keeping the packet out of the water with the other. He
knew it . . . Of course he had taken the money! How much
was there? Were they really bills? Despite the darkness, he
had been able to make out that they were bills—not little
ones, big ones! He would have been willing to swear on his
own head that they were bills. Bills look like nothing else,
besides other bills—and not little ones like you see in the
hands of the minor Black shopkeepers . . . No! Big ones,
thick and hard, and crackling, and large. Yeah! How many
were there?

Then he didn't think about anything specific. In his
mind, things were blurring together, getting mixed up; everything was competing with everything else. He wanted to
hope but didn't dare. He had learned not to hope too soon.
His heart was beating fast.

He got to the canoe and climbed in. The image of his
fiancée crossed his mind: he froze with surprise. That habit
of thinking of one thing while doing another. He pulled
himself together. He was wrong to hope. One mustn't be
so quick to believe. But as much as he said this, he still did.

He looked to all sides, suspiciously. Perhaps someone was
crouching somewhere in the bushes? One never knew . . .
Apparently satisfied after this rapid inspection, he stuffed
the little packet of bills into the pocket of his spare shorts. If
only he knew how much was there. He chose a discreet spot

under the cover of the bush to lay down his fine clothes, including the shorts that held the bills. He wondered what he would do with the other clothes, the ones that were dirty and wet. ok! So he would sink them. That's it, he was going to sink them . . . That was a good idea . . .

He was naked; he climbed into the boat, taking with him the dirty clothes, and leaving the other ones on the bank. For a moment he hesitated. Perhaps it wasn't prudent to leave the money like that—perhaps someone was hiding somewhere . . . What could he do? What might happen to the packet of bills? . . . Who could be hiding around here? Did that person know that Banda would come here tonight? No, nothing would happen.

He paddled. The canoe forced its way through the water of the river widthwise. Arriving at the middle, Banda jumped into the water, took hold of one edge of the canoe and pressed down on it with all his might. Water rushed into the carved-out space in the log. In a few seconds the boat sank straight down, taking with it the attached clothing.

For a moment he contemplated the paddle that was drifting away in the current: it would be far from here by daybreak; he felt a touch of nostalgia. He swam back to shore . . .

Back on the bank he rubbed himself at length from head to foot. Then he moved about, shaking his arms and legs. When he felt dry enough, he dressed himself: he put on his shorts and his khaki shirt. He instinctively put his hand into the right pocket of the shorts: it was empty! This realization sent shivers down his spine. He'd been wrong to leave his money like that . . . Still he had thought about it. What could have happened? Could it have happened? His hand drove down into his left pocket and ran into the little humid bundle. Ah! No, nothing had happened: the money was there. He nervously removed the packet from his pocket and proceeded to squeeze it, to assess it by tossing it around in his hand. It was as thick as when he left. He wanted to undo the piece of cloth: he stopped suddenly—what was the point, since he would never be able to count the money in the dark? He carefully jammed it deep down back into his pocket. He made sure it wouldn't come out, that it wouldn't fall out, even if something happened, even if he had to run . . . One never knew: anything could happen.

He was getting ready to leave. He had been facing away from the river up to that point; instinctively he turned to look at it. He stared at it insistently and with melancholy. Perhaps he wanted to be sure that it would keep his secret: there are moments in life when one can't help but give a human spirit to anything that moves. Perhaps he was simply looking at what had been the theater of his despair, completing, in the process, his first pilgrimage.

Once again, he cast an aggressively suspicious glance all about him. But no, nobody was there. Why be afraid? Never had he thought he could be so unnecessarily afraid. Making sure to be quiet, he crept through the bushes along the bank and just as quickly found himself on the road. He set out for Bamila.

A rooster crowed . . .

10

BANDA WALKED SLOWLY, without haste, his bare feet skirting the road's familiar stones. He wound his way along the long-loading dock. He could see logs lying here and there like dead bodies: they were grey in the night. There was a light, either in the nearby train station or in the sawmill yard. South Tanga was sleeping the sleep of the blessed; it did so with goodwill and a moving, edifying serenity. When he was on the bridge, he leaned over the railing, looking into the darkness, trying to make out Koumé's body, knowing that it lay down below. Since he couldn't, he began walking again.

From time to time he shivered, his whole body shook; the air had suddenly cooled. Dawn was near. He wasn't thinking about anything in particular. He was simply walking, like a robot. His big feet were striking the gravelly roadway—already dusty despite the previous night's rain. He wasn't thinking about anything in particular: too many possible topics were simultaneously available for his consideration. He shivered frequently. Sometimes his teeth chattered because of the sudden cold.

He crossed the paths of people dressed in their Sunday best, but he didn't notice, his consciousness didn't register their presence. He felt as though his bodily organs were functioning in slow motion. Even his step was weighed down and uncertain. He reacted a second late. He had become exhausted without noticing, had expected too much of his own strength. A group of adolescents brought him back to reality. They weren't speaking, and it looked as if they were taking particular pleasure in listening to the muffled rumble of their own disorganized and heavy stomping. Banda knew that children of that age were usually loud. He wondered why they said nothing. They weren't carrying anything. They were also rushing ahead in an unexpected way. He stopped thinking about the adolescents even though their silence surprised him.

Then he crossed the women's paths; he saw them. They weren't carrying packs; they were walking arms akimbo and were even wearing brightly colored dresses. He didn't understand them right away. But the women, who walked in little clusters, were speaking in low voices. From one group he could make out little pieces of conversation, like little puffs of wind. They were speaking of a roadblock, of shots fired, of boys sought after, of a White man who had died at the hospital, of arrests, of a mass, of communion . . . And as he walked he realized that it wasn't a single group that had said all of those things, but many groups whose paths he had crossed one after another. He had forgotten the roadblocks and the fact that it was Sunday morning. Those people—were going to mass! "Ah! . . . I understand." He must be really tired.

He was too late to go through the roadblock, especially because of the direction in which he was travelling. He couldn't continue toward Bamila on the road. They would think his wanting to leave the city at that hour meant he was trying to escape, and they would certainly detain him. He could not continue toward Bamila on the road. A shortcut through the forest? There were many . . . He was weary. But he pulled himself together; he wasn't going to lose his concentration now. Anything could happen at any time.

He gave himself little blows on the back of the head to wake himself up. He was encountering more and more people. They were all abnormally quiet. They walked without haste. Those people, they must be true believers, he thought. To come from so far away to attend mass, the sacred mass at Tanga! And at night! Oh! It's true that if I were a Christian, I would also attend the morning mass, that way at least you had the rest of Sunday off. Yes! But to come from so far away, just to attend mass, that surprises me. To walk ten or fifteen kilometers at night, just for that . . . Hey! Why not? That's it, that's what I'm going to do. That's a good idea . . . All of a sudden, he thought of the little bundle, quivered, then stopped suddenly. He nervously felt his thigh where the pocket was. Ah! It was there. There was no danger that it would get lost. Yes! That's what I'll do. I'll backtrack and go to mass; the Catholic mission isn't far from here. And early in the day I'll go through the roadblocks with the others . . . And why not? Will someone be able to pick me out? Who would be able to do that? That person would be really gifted. Ah, yes, that's a good idea: I'm going to attend mass, I'll go through the roadblock at daybreak just to see if they pick me out . . . But I know they won't. And by then maybe they'll have discovered the body. Yeah! Maybe they'll have discovered the body by daybreak when I go through the roadblock . . . I'm curious to see what happens.

He nonchalantly turned around and began walking in step with a group of men and women, people who were coming from the forest. They were coming from the forest just to attend mass! Yesterday they were working, exhausting themselves in their fields, and already they were thinking about it. They were thinking that they would rise early, at the first rooster's crow, so that they could go to the Catholic mission in Tanga. They would make sure that they were there before six o'clock so that they could attend the whole thing, and not just part of it. That's what he didn't understand. He could hear them speaking in low voices. They were talking about the young mechanic and the White man, Mr. T. Several times he almost interjected, "Hey, that's not right! That's not what happened! You've been misinformed. They've lied to you. That's not true. Please listen,

I know the story well, I know the full story because . . ."
It was with great effort that he held back. He walked with
them all the way to the Catholic mission, all the way to the
church, crossing the threshold with them. At no point did
they guess that he wasn't one of them.

It had been a very long time since he'd attended mass.
He was delighted at the idea of going this morning. It would
have been hard to tell what he expected: perhaps a whiff
of his childhood, a forgotten smell? Suddenly, he remembered the period when his mother dragged him to mass
every Sunday. He was only an adolescent at the time. His
mother, for her part, had been a Christian for a number of
years, since her husband's death. She was pious, went to
confession and communion at Easter, paid her tithe without fail, went to midnight mass on Christmas, and, her lips
moving, recited the rosary every evening. He was not the
offspring of a Catholic family: therefore he had to wait until
he could correctly recite his catechism before being properly
baptized. His mother did nothing but press him to learn it
by heart—she had bought him a very pretty illustrated edition. She pressured him constantly to attend the courses of
an eminent catechist from the mission—it was said his students never failed the baptism exam. She wanted nothing
more than to see him baptized.

In reality, getting him to accomplish this proved difficult. The adolescent did not live with his mother—he rarely
lived near her. Moreover, he had been enrolled in a public
school. In short, like most students his age, six out of seven
days, he escaped the authority of the church. Only on Sat-
urdays did his mother appear; then, she would inevitably
pose this question:

"Did you attend mass on the first Friday of the month,
my son? Did you eat meat yesterday?"

Or again:

"Did you go listen to the catechist, son?"

The young boy paid little attention to the priests, the Latin songs, the choirboys, and the catechists; it turned out that
he also had an astonishing aptitude for the bold-faced lie.

"Of course, Mother. Of course I went," he would answer.
Or again:

"Mother, I was so sick! I couldn't. No, Mother, I really couldn't. It's not that I didn't have the will or the desire, I assure you. But I was so sick! I couldn't go, Mother, no, I really couldn't . . ."

The mother knew her son; she knew she couldn't take his declarations at face value. But how could she check? (It should be noted that at the time the woman showed a degree of faith few people could appreciate. Given how far Bamila was from Tanga, she could have attended mass every other Sunday—the bishop had even authorized it! But she had forced herself to come to Tanga every Saturday, although it wasn't clear whether this was to see her son or to attend Sunday mass. The two must have been equally important. Whatever the reason, the result was that she never missed the opportunity to drag him off to mass, often by force, with Banda trying to escape.)

The first—and only!—time that she had asked Banda's uncle, the tailor, about the young man's diligence in the rituals of piety, the man had responded with impatience. He had never been baptized, he said; he added that he had no intention of ever being baptized, and he wasn't any the worse for it. Wasn't the best way to raise a child to feed him and leave him be? Let him run around or sleep or laugh or cry when he feels like it: that's the best way to raise a kid, especially a boy. (In reality, the tailor had an inexplicable weak spot for his nephew, and he showed considerable indulgence toward the conduct of this overly wild boy—and the least one could say is that it was rarely without reproach. One might even think he was encouraging this behavior. This led to an almost unbreakable bond between them that grew stronger by the day.) At the most, he could accept that the boy be put in school to learn the White man's language; after all, those folks ruled the world. But the catechism, mass, the rosary, confession, morning and evening prayer, and all the other whims, what the hell did that all add up to? His sister acted as if religion were something new . . . And their ancestors, those who had lived in a country without White men, or missionaries, or nuns, or churches, or bells, who lived before the arrival of Whites, didn't they believe in God? He wanted to know, why it was necessary to wet your head with a little water, to kneel before a priest, to go swallow a breadcrumb without chewing it, in order to believe in God. And suppose she wanted to make her son a priest . . . Ah! Now that wouldn't be a bad idea at all. That was a well-paid profession. He had seen indigenous priests, and up close. They were certainly the most privileged among the Blacks: brick houses, tables that were waited upon just like for a White man, motorbikes, bicycles—they certainly had those things. And the respect and admiration of everyone, even the Whites! So let's just suppose she was going to turn her boy into a priest, that wouldn't be a bad idea. But then she should come out and say it! Let's have it out so we know where we stand. Only he didn't believe that boys like Banda were priest material—certainly not. Or he knew nothing about children.

After her brother's forceful declaration on the matter, the distraught mother had seriously thought of enrolling her son in the missionary school. But she was warned that children learned little there besides the catechism and Latin songs and that she would have to pay a substantial tuition every year. In the meantime, Banda had tried to pass a catechism exam in order to be baptized: his results were so poor that they preferred to drop the subject. The mother kept her son enrolled in the public school to honor her husband's intentions, despite the pressures of one of her relations who was a catechist. She also began to have other ambitions for her son besides those relating specifically to religious practice and his eternal salvation.

When he returned to Bamila, much taller and entirely independent, emancipated, in sum, it became even harder to keep Banda in touch with God . . . for obvious reasons. And in fact, as soon as he could, he refused all guidance in that regard—he had never had any penchant for theology. The catechist, the same one as before, had in the meantime become lukewarm about religion, or at least tempered his previously rigorous conceptions, and he made it his responsibility to reassure Banda's mother. Wasn't her son grown up? How could she still be responsible for him? Besides, God was infinitely merciful, and would send his grace at some point, if only at Banda's deathbed.

The mother and son, having established that they would never agree on religious matters, bonded over other things. Indeed, it was around that time that she began to feel the symptoms of that unidentified and incurable disease that would progressively drive her into almost total confinement. Except for religious matters, the young man was willing to make every concession for his sick mother: that's what was strange about their relationship.

Perhaps, at a time when he wasn't aware of it, an enemy of her religion had influenced him. Or perhaps, like his uncle who had never gotten bored of the spectacle of the street, he was simply too drawn by the whirlwind of tangible realities.

When he entered the church, it was still completely dark. Only the light of a candle flickered over there on the altar. Despite the hour, the many faithful already filled the body of the church. They were reciting the rosary in unison, men and women. He could only make out the main words . . . *Maaaaaria . . . Graaaaatia . . . Yeeesus . . . Maria . . . Gratia . . . Yesus;* he couldn't make out what they were saying in between. They really only took pleasure in emphasizing Maria, Gratia, Yesus; they didn't articulate the rest. The prayer, recited in this manner, resembled a strange chant, a funereal song, boring and sad, where the same musical phrase would be repeated endlessly. This gave the church a sleepy air. As a result, here and there a head was nodding; a man over there was starting to doze.

Banda took his place in the central aisle, on the long wooden bench. He leaned against a pillar. He began to daydream, while the faithful recited the rosary: *Maria . . . Gratia . . . Yesus . . . Maria . . . Gratia . . . Yesus.* Suddenly, they were quiet; they had worked the entire rosary. They waited in silence for the mass to begin. Coughs answered each other, echoing in repetition. It's incredible how much a group of men can cough! Banda thought.

The left half, exclusively reserved for women, soon drew his attention. Without even considering the sound of wailing babies, there arose from this part of the church a permanent, dull, tumultuous hum. The verger needed all the authority he could muster, his power and his regalia, to maintain any sense of order there: to be honest, the women's sector was enough to attract all of his ardor and professional dedication. This also meant that those on the men's side could devote themselves, without fear or scruples, to the pleasures of sleep. Dawn rapidly invaded the church and the women discovered one another. They examined each other with circumspection at first, then with haughtiness or indifference, or again with hostility. The young women in particular had a hard time disguising their feelings. It was clear that this one hated that one who was wearing a prettier dress, and she magisterially scorned anyone who didn't have a dress whose beauty, price, and cut were equal to her own. Banda observed that nothing can be meaner than a woman. Few graciously accepted to move over a bit in order to create space for a recent arrival. There were even a few shoving matches, unfortunately, to Banda's taste, of little consequence; he was starting to have fun. When the verger appeared everything automatically calmed down, while behind him other arguments broke out, other voices could be heard . . .

The bell rang. The real mass was beginning. The priest and the choirboys kneeled before the altar in an attitude of absolute respect and humble submission, heads bent to their chests as they recited the prayers in Latin. You could hear their voices all the way to the doors: *Confiteor Deo omnipotenti . . . Amen . . . Dominus vobiscum . . . Et cum spiritutuo . . .* Who will ever tell me what the words *Dominus vobiscum cum spiritutuo* mean? thought Banda. One day, the catechist admitted to me that even he didn't know. True, he also added that this was of no importance whatsoever. But I would like to know. I would like to know the meaning of: *Dominus vobis-cum cum spritutuo* . . .

Suddenly a whining voice began a song that was joined at the chorus by the entire congregation. The faithful kneeled in two steps. Banda stayed seated. Memories rushed by as he took in the soft, sweet, melodious, lingering notes escaping from the harmonium over his head. Once again, he could see his mother: young, beautiful, her face radiant, her expression joyful, speaking to the eminent catechist, graciously saluting a friend. He could hear her thin tuneful voice. He put his face in his hands; he thought he was going to cry. It felt as if his mother, his real mother, had been dead for years. The one who was sick over there in Bamila looked so little like the other one, the real one, the beautiful one. It was as if his mother had been taken from him and another one substituted while he wasn't paying attention.

Suddenly, he jammed his hand into the left pocket of his khaki shorts, raised his head and looked around as if afraid he was being watched. The little humid bundle was in its place. Oh! There was no risk of its getting lost. After all, it had stayed in Koumé's pocket! How stupid to be afraid like this. If only he could know how much money was in the bundle . . . If only he could know. He grew more and more sleepy. He buried his head in his hands again while his elbows rested on his knees . . .

He only woke up a half hour later. Someone was tapping his shoulder, softly but insistently. He raised his head and saw the verger.

"If you knew you hadn't slept enough last night," the verger reproached him quietly, "if you knew it, why did you come to mass today? Who was forcing you?"

Banda swelled up:

"Does the Good Lord also forbid sleeping?"

It was a classic reply in his situation. Nevertheless, upon hearing this, a young boy behind him had to suppress a fit of laughter. He turned around and smiled at the exact replica of the kid he had been, always looking for an excuse to laugh.

"The Good Lord may not forbid sleeping," the verger answered. "In any case, he doesn't recommend drinking Saturday night or sleeping with other people's wives . . ."

"Well, that's very interesting! How do you know that I sleep with other people's wives?" Banda asked, loud enough to be heard by quite a few people and as if he had recognized the truth of the first accusation.

"All one has to do is look at you," the verger snapped back; "all someone has to do is look at you to see that that's what you do with your life . . ."

"And what if I had my own wife?"

"You? Hah! . . . I'll bet you anything that you don't have your own wife, anything you want, that you don't have your own wife. Besides, even if you did, she wouldn't be enough for you . . ."

The verger moved away, a little sheepishly; he didn't want to cause a scandal; the altercation had generated a buzz around Banda who was enjoying himself more and more. Strangely, this entire atmosphere was causing him to go back in time.

A priest, a missionary, was now standing at the pulpit. They were all listening to him very carefully; Banda, too, was watching him. It felt as if he were seeing all these characters for the very first time: up until that moment, he had only seen them with a child's eyes. The missionary began speaking while pretending to read the book. After a while, he shut it.

Banda refused to listen to him; he would rather have thought of something else. The man spoke his language so poorly! At the beginning he was shocked by it, at this man speaking his language with such disdain, but then he was amused. If the priest had only known that once a minute he was saying something horrible!

He touched his thigh near the pocket and felt the little humid bundle. How much could it be?

The missionary's speech was about men's duty to love one another. As he spoke, a jerky and comical motion animated his long beard.

So, if one were to believe him, men were supposed to love one another. How so? Here, he began a long dissertation on the Good Samaritan, even though it wasn't Good Samaritan Sunday. Banda knew it well. Oh! If he knew one story, it was that one. What Banda couldn't understand was why more importance should be accorded to the Good Samaritan who treated the wounded man than to the wounded man himself. To Banda, it was the man who had been attacked and wounded by the thieves who had the greatest dramatic interest, the greatest emotional possibility. Whereas the Good Samaritan, who cared! Couldn't any woman in Bamila heal a wounded man? Hey! He said to himself, it's as if more importance were given to me than to Koumé. For, at the end of the day, I am more like the Good Samaritan and Koumé the victim of the thieves . . . Hey! Yes, that's true. And how could you give me more importance than Koumé? Besides, I wasn't even able to save him. And I'm certain that the Good Samaritan didn't save his wounded man either. The wounded man is the real tough guy: the Good Samaritan had it easy!

Another proof of one's love for one's neighbor, the missionary continued, is to respect what belongs to him—what belongs to one's neighbor. Did not Jesus, the master of us all, live on this earth? And despite being poor did he ever touch the belongings of another? Think of how much misery, how many quarrels, disputes, debates, would be avoided if people imitated the example of our Lord Jesus Christ in their daily lives! But instead, what do they do? They sleep with other people's wives. They beat their bosses and steal their money. Don't they care about the young Jesus' years of apprenticeship in his father Joseph's workshop?

Banda's ears perked up. The missionary was going to speak about Koumé—he knew it. He could feel it coming. The crowd had become almost silent; you couldn't even hear coughing. People were waiting to be informed: it was clear that they desperately wanted that.

It was the duty of every Christian worthy of the name, the priest continued, to reveal, if he knew it, the whereabouts of the young man Koumé who had attacked his boss. All the country's Christians knew and respected Mr. T. because of his generosity toward the Catholic mission. Well, this saintly man had just passed away at the hospital, because of the cruel blows he had received from Koumé and the other young men. But Koumé was the real person responsible, in a word, the leader. If someone here knew where Koumé was hidden . . . After mass, he, the reverend Father Kolmann, would take on the duty of hearing that information, and in private. Let that person reveal it, for the love of Christ and all men. Never mind that civil law severely punishes "tacit complicity" (which he said in French), which is to say . . .

But already, Banda was no longer listening. Anyway, the priest didn't go on for much longer. Just as fast, people rushed toward the door. Banda deliberately joined the crowd.

Outside he could breathe more freely—or so he thought. He cocked his head without really knowing why. He had the same feeling as a day earlier, when the regional guards were taking him to the police station. As if a battle had been forced on him that he was destined to lose. It was also as if, while he had been sleeping, he had been carried out of his familiar universe, into a world that was not his own, where everything was backward. A real nightmare . . .

Lost in the crowd, he felt some degree of security, though, out of fear of thieves, he kept his hand in his pocket to protect the bundle of bills. He only regretted that the others were so sad. He didn't like to see an unhappy crowd. After all, why were they sad? Why? It's true that they were forest people for the most part; yes, that's where they came from. The inhabitants of Tanga never came to mass in the morning—they preferred the daytime, which was better suited to the display of sumptuous attire. Here, it was the forest people, generally more sensitive, too sensitive, and at this particular moment they were a little lost. They were mostly just wondering what was going on. Banda couldn't see that if they looked sad, more than anything, they were perplexed: they simply didn't understand. The crowd moved along the road silently and without haste. The sight of the children, who ran, yelled, roughhoused, jostled each other, comforted the young man: at least they weren't worried.

All of a sudden, a noise rose from the front of the crowd, traveling from one part to another with a discretion and speed incomprehensible to anyone who is unfamiliar with the forest people as they were at the time of this story. The body of the young mechanic had just been discovered under the bridge. They rushed along, freed from the pressing apprehension, not to say terror that, because of Koumé, had struck the region since yesterday afternoon. Banda didn't follow them at first. What good would it do? he thought to himself . . . But he changed his mind. Ah! No, he thought, that isn't prudent. I have to go, I have to run along with them, I have to be like everybody else. Someone might wonder why he showed so little curiosity: you never knew who was a policeman in this country, and especially who wasn't. You never knew . . . And he ran.

Near the bridge a covered vehicle, a police car, was parked. Some hundred territorial guards who had arrived the night before—precipitously called up from the garrisons in Tanga after the events had transpired—were keeping the crowd at bay by brandishing the stocks of their rifles in front of them. The crowd was shaken by murmurs, whispers, and necks were craned. This is how Banda learned that the body had already been carried into the long covered car next to which a half dozen high-ranking White officers were gravely speaking, in low voices, with gestures that Banda thought indicated their indecision; it amused him.

He still had one hand in his pocket to protect the bills. What could the White men be saying to each other? He would have given anything to find out. He expected the officers to suddenly point to him, take him from the crowd. At every instant he was waiting for it, even though he was aware that they couldn't know, that they wouldn't come to get him. At the same time, he couldn't help offering up a secret challenge: if Whites were as smart as they say, well let them find me on their own. Let them figure out exactly what happened . . . Go ahead if you're so smart. What are you waiting for? Come and grab me. I'm here in this crowd; I'm tall, very dark-skinned. I'm wearing khaki canvas clothes, I have a scar on my chin, I have big eyes that seem to be bugging out of my head . . . And despite all that you can't find me? It really did seem that the White officers would never find him. Besides, he told himself, I'm not really the one they're after.

After half an hour, two White ranked officers got into the front of the covered car and headed out; four others who were on motorcycles with sidecars followed them. The crowd parted automatically to let the three vehicles pass, and then it closed up again around the territorial guards who were setting up in columns, revealing their own desire to leave as well. But the crowd that encircled them like a vise did not part. Instead, they were shouting out invective at them, as varied as they were unexpected.

"Cannibals . . . Murderers . . . You killed him! You were willing to kill your brother! Aren't you ashamed? Your brother! Savages! Pack of bloodthirsty animals! Dangerous beasts! Sellouts! . . . Traitors! Stateless thugs! Defectors!"

Some were even throwing stones: it was probably adolescents, those precipitous in their passion and anger, and perhaps also the women, who were always willing to engage in all sorts of provocation when they felt their men were nearby.

The territorial guards, men from the North, were tall, strong, and unflappable. Without needing orders, they formed a compact, massive square, put their bayonets on their rifles, and advanced resolutely without saying a word: they must have been well trained. They appeared unfazed by the stones. They advanced by creating a path with the tips of their bayonets. The men in their path backed away hesitatingly at first. But when it became clear that the territorial guards in their irresistible march would let nothing stop their forward momentum, there was a stampede to escape, with cries and moans, insults hurled and unnamable curses.

A few more stones were tossed. Without even turning around, the guards moved away in that massive, compact square that might remind one of a rock against which the waters of a river would persist in beating to no avail.

Banda once again took the road to Bamila. What are they going to do with the body? he wondered. What are they going to do, that's what I'd like to know . . . Does Fort-Nègre look like Tanga? I'd really like to know the answer to that question: Is Fort-Nègre like Tanga?

11

MORE OR LESS HALFWAY between the city and Bamila, Banda stopped. There were no huts in sight: to the left and right, nothing but the bush or the forest.

He sat on the low embankment that ran along the road and exhaled. It felt as if he were back in friendly territory. Sweat beaded on his face: he wiped it with the palm of his wide hand, and then dried it off on his khaki shorts. It feels good to be in the forest! the young man thought naïvely. Why did he want to go to the city later? And maybe he was wrong? He had often felt how cruel and hard the city was, with its White officers, its regional guards, its territorial guards with bayonets fixed to their barrels, its one-way streets, and its "no natives allowed" policy. But this time, he had been its victim: he had realized everything that was inhuman about it.

Sighing, he brought his hand to his black eye: the swelling had diminished since last night. And perhaps Fort-Nègre wasn't like Tanga? Perhaps Tanga was a special case? And perhaps the ferocious and recalcitrant personality of the inhabitants of this area explained the extreme harshness of the Whites? Was everywhere really like Tanga? He'd have to find out. He'd have given a lot to know. One way or another he couldn't continue living in Bamila after his mother died. You can't live in a large village like Bamila where all the old men hate you and you hate them. You can't even live in one of the nearby villages because their hate will pursue you . . .

In fact, he had already decided to leave Bamila. Still, he had no more reason to do so than any number of other young people, and they could have complained about the area but never left. In fact, he said precisely that to himself: but after a long process of consideration mostly motivated by pride and lack of respect for his neighbors, he arrived at the rather hasty conclusion that they simply lacked the will, or they really didn't know what they wanted. If he had been able to look at himself more clearly—but that was impossible—he would have noted that what was impelling him was mostly a force beyond him, a sort of existence outside himself and even Bamila, one amplified by his temperament and his past.

I won't be able to live in Bamila any longer, he thought bitterly. Still, it's sad . . . Yes, in a way it's really sad . . . Is Fort-Nègre just another Tanga? If he could just live in Bamila after his mother's death. But this idea repulsed him just as much. Didn't that mean compromising with people like Tonga? You can't live constantly on the warpath: wouldn't that mean concessions of a kind he wasn't used to?

He contemplated the yellow bush in front of him, and beyond that, the dark green, compact and motionless forest. It reminded him of a night during the hot season when there isn't a breath of air. He didn't feel anything precise: he was neither happy nor sad. He only felt tired, very tired. He hadn't slept in two days. He also realized with stupor that he hadn't eaten. He was happy he hadn't realized it earlier: it would have discouraged him. Now, he encouraged himself by noting that soon he would be able to satisfy all of his bodily needs: just acknowledging this calmed them.

He touched his thigh in the area of the pocket and felt the money. He slipped his hand into his shorts; his fingers ran into the packet of bills and remained clasped around it. While he felt the bills, his ears caught the far-off purr of a motor. Instinctively, he jerked his hand out and stood up. He resembled a nervous animal. In fact, why was he leaving himself exposed to the gaze of anybody who might happen along? He looked around anxiously. You never know, he told himself; these days you can't tell what will happen in this godforsaken country. If someone had, at that particular moment, been able to calmly observe Banda, he would have thought that the henchmen of Tanga were tracking him for some unspeakable crime.

Son, things are going badly, his uncle used to say.

The insistent purr of the engine was rapidly getting closer. He noticed a dense thicket not too far from the road and he jumped into it. No sooner had he hidden and turned back to look at the road than a large car passed by like a rocket. He thought he had spied two Whites, of both sexes, but beyond that he didn't think much of it (he would see the car again several times that day). A thick cloud of red dust swirled above the roadbed. Banda was panting. Damn! Couldn't he get rid of this fear? Why was he afraid? In any case, nobody knows where I am or what happened. So why am I afraid? He could have asked himself this question all day and would never have been able to answer it.

He stayed in the thicket for a long time in front of the cloud of dust that took its time in dissipating; his gaze was lost in the distance. He heard the sound of the engine move away and disappear. He swallowed. He felt a cold sweat travel down his spine. Damn, why was he afraid like that? Would he ever be able to get rid of this fear?

Once more, he pushed his hand into his left pocket; he wrapped his nervous fingers around the packet of bills and fiddled with it nervously. He took his hand out and then dug it in again. How much could it be? Perhaps a lot. The packet was so fat . . . And the bills were large and thick and crackled under his touch, just like the ones you see at the Greek merchants'. He removed his hand and just as quickly reinserted it again. As he indulged in this strange little ritual, his imagination wandered through a series of scabrous associations. He thus rediscovered the notion of providence about which he had been told in a rare catechism course he had actually attended: but he just as quickly rejected this idea of providence, their providence. After what he had heard during mass this morning, was he going to start believing their stories? No! It must instead be—his father, yes, his departed father! Banda's fate must finally have caused his father to pity him. It's true, his father couldn't remain indifferent to his misfortune: no, he couldn't. Aren't the dead always present among the living? Aren't they spotted sometimes? Didn't they get mixed up in the affairs of the living? It was natural that his misfortunes should move his departed father. How could he not have thought about this precious and constant resource earlier, about his father's love and solicitude?

He remembered a troubling story—all the more troubling in that it was true—that had happened to one of his mother's neighbors. The illness of her only son was causing this woman great anguish: in a word, she was desperate. Well, one night, in her sleep, her mother-in-law and her husband, both dead, visited her. They indicated an herb as a cure that grew not far from the family hut. At dawn, drunk with hope, the mother discovered the herb indicated in the dream. The little boy was thereby snatched back from an almost certain death.

Curiously, he had always thought that his father would end up doing something for him. And now it had happened. Wasn't life full of surprises?

But just as quickly, he was overwhelmed with thoughts that were, paradoxically, all the more bitter. He was still standing in the thicket, staring into the distance, while his fingers fiddled with the little packet. And what if he were really cursed the way those in Bamila said? Losing two hundred kilos of cacao at once isn't something that you forget; and it doesn't happen to everybody. If you thought about it, this money he had in his pocket . . . well, in truth it didn't belong to him; he was going to steal it—it wasn't his money . . . he was taking it from someone. Had he ever been able to accomplish anything on his own? All alone he would never get married; he wouldn't be able to wed that girl. Yeah! That was true; alone he would never marry. Without Koumé . . . without the death of Koumé. Now Koumé, that was a tough guy.

Try as he may, he couldn't convince himself that he wasn't wrong in taking this money, in appropriating it. It was his right, as long as he wasn't wronging anyone and he needed it. Still, a bitter taste lingered in his mouth. Maybe it was true that he was cursed, a good-for-nothing incapable of doing anything by himself. Why, then, go to the city if all he was going to do was fail? He'd do just as well not going. He was starting to really lose confidence in himself. Rarely had growing pains been so sharp.

Damn! These are all stupid thoughts, he concluded. If I take this money, it would only be fair. Still, he didn't really believe that: but in his case, it was much less about morality than pride.

He had therefore decided that the money would belong to him. Slowly, he took the hand from his pocket holding the little packet that he brought before his eyes. He was holding it firmly in his left hand, while clumsily trying to undo it with his right hand. His hands were trembling and his open mouth let his lower lip droop, as if he were in the grip of a severe episode of malaria. Completely unaware of all this, he finally squatted on the grass, which he spread with his hands, thereby creating a little clearing. He made a violent effort to control his emotions and began counting the bills. How many could there be? What a stupid question! Wasn't he about to find out? Wasn't he going to know in a second? One . . . Two . . . Three . . . Yeah! These were thousand franc bills! My God: These were thousand franc bills! How many were there? He started over again. One . . . Two . . . Three . . . And what if they were counterfeit? And what if they were fakes . . . There were so many in circulation, or so people said. What a thought! Would Mr. T. have stocked counterfeit bills? How? First, he would realize that they were fakes: he wouldn't accept them. And then, even if he had realized this only later, he would have passed them on to others, to Greeks who don't understand anything about anything. Mr. T. was a real Frenchman, educated and everything; on top of that he wasn't stupid . . . He had gotten his numbers mixed up again . . . Would he ever succeed in counting properly? That habit of thinking about one thing while doing another!

He started over again, his teeth clenched, his lips pursed. One . . . Two . . . Three . . . Four . . . Five . . . Six . . . Seven! Eight! Nine! Ten! Eleven! Twelve! Thirteen! Fourteen! Fifteen!!!!! Fifteen thousand francs! Fifteen thousand! Fifteen! Yeah. That wasn't possible. He must have made a mistake, a huge mistake. He was petrified. No, he must have made a mistake: there had to be a mistake. Was his eyesight blurry? Perhaps. He was so tired. He rubbed his eyes violently applying his large palm to them. He started again, his teeth clenched, his lips pursed, squinting, frowning. One . . . Two . . . Three . . . Four . . . Five . . . Six . . . Seven . . . Eight! Nine! Ten! Eleven! Twelve! Thirteen! Fourteen! Fifteen!!!!! No doubt about it; it was fifteen thousand francs. Were they really thousand franc notes? He carefully inspected each piece of paper. Yes, these were thousand franc notes. Yeah! More than enough to get married with, much more than he needed . . . No doubt that his father showed him the way. Just to prove to him that one should never get discouraged. In life, one must never get discouraged, he thought. You always have to fight, nobody knows when luck will appear one day, you just find it by rummaging around.

He had to make an effort to get control of himself: he felt faint. He feverishly laid the bills one on top the other and rolled them back up in the piece of cloth. He put the little packet back in the very bottom of his pocket. At that point he rose to his feet: something cracked in the joints of his legs; he noticed that they hurt because he had been squatting for too long. He went back to the roadway and began walking with purpose.

His survival instinct was on heightened alert. While he crossed the village, he walked in the middle of the road, as if wanting to keep his distance from other men. This is what an assassin or anyone else in possession of an important secret does. Didn't he, in fact, have a secret? He was surprised to find himself walking in the middle of the roadway like this and was afraid he might give himself away with his extreme cautiousness. He decided to relax; he made an effort to wear an easygoing indifference. He even forced himself to whistle:

Had you offered me a dress would I have said that
   you were stingy?
You are handsome, and Black, like a black snake
   lying in a manioc field.
You are handsome, slender as a corn stalk.
Whatever you do I know you understood my winking.
I'll wait for you along the narrow path, at half past five.
For you I'll bear all, contempt, other's opprobrium,
   beatings, torture, and even flight.
You stole my heart, the one you keep and refuse to
   give back.

That had been his poor mother's song back when she was young and beautiful, when she could sing and still take part in the pleasures of life. My mother was beautiful back then, he thought, beautiful and radiant. She never got tired of joking and laughing, and when she laughed her teeth were white.

Walking in the street, as he crossed the town, he could hear songs, laughter, bursts of conversation coming from the huts. Apparently, some people were happy with their lives. He was jealous. Still, six kilometers wasn't that far from the city: no doubt they had heard about it. But those people didn't worry—they never worried. How? By drinking perhaps? But in his case, it was precisely when he was drinking that he least forgot what was going on around him—or so he thought!

At the time, there were still, in all the villages, even those located on the road, a category of people for whom the Greek merchants, or the White officers, or the regional or territorial guards, or Mr. T. didn't exist. In sum, these were people for whom Tanga didn't exist, or existed so little that it just wasn't a concern. They ignored the city—sometimes deliberately, but usually without forethought—and didn't go there. For them, the world was limited to their village, or more exactly to the surrounding forest. They spent the whole day in the forest. When they weren't working their fields, they were there to drink palm wine in peace or to hunt or to engage in activities that the law deemed unacceptable and for which the forest provided its maternal protection. The most consistent characteristics of this particular category of humanity were its good humor, its boasting, and the consistency of its feelings over the long term. Crossing the village, Banda could hear them singing in their huts—because it was Sunday, and on Sundays the regional guards' and White officers' incursions were rare. He wondered how they did it, how they could worry about nothing, not even what was happening right then in Tanga, only six kilometers away.

A man had come down onto the road behind him; he was following Banda and walking with an uneven gait; he was singing in a thick and high-pitched voice. Banda made sure not to turn around though he recognized him as an acquaintance. That didn't keep the man from calling out, "Friend . . . Friend . . . Friend! Who are you to not even turn around when you're called? Don't you want a little of our good palm wine? Answer me. Don't disdain my wine, I beg you. Today, we've decided to offer it to any stranger we like who should happen to walk along this road . . . Oh! You know, if you miss this opportunity, it's just your loss. In any case, the closest village is Bamila; and they won't offer you wine in Bamila, believe me. Heh heh heh. Don't count on them for that; you would be asking too much, heh heh heh. They lack in hospitality over there. I've heard it's that they're overly jealous about their women, heh heh heh . . ."

He would have liked to decline this invitation, but he didn't. He might have let his secret out. The man who was now taking long strides finally caught him.

He turned around and the other man recognized him immediately, and began protesting:

"Hey! But . . . it's Banda! Well, my brother, how are you?"

"Neither good nor bad . . ."

"Yeah, hey, you'd disappeared, huh?"

"How can you say I disappeared when you're the one who's always gone? Where could you possibly be going like that?"

"I leave you the road, I prefer the forest: first, it's always cool there, and besides the trees are my great friends. To be frank, trees are the best, the surest, hosts for those who know them . . . Say brother, what's up with you? You would have just walked on by without even saying hi to your old friends? Banda, strange things are happening . . . Sometimes I wonder where things are headed. Tell me, where's this world going, your world? When dealing with your family and friends you behave like their enemy. You get rich with your cacao and your Greeks, you kill the Whites . . . Life is strange, isn't it? Hey, don't you look dressed up? Do you have a girlfriend in town? The city sure suits some people . . ."

Banda told him that the day before he had seen his two hundred kilos of cacao thrown on the fire. The other knit his brow and became thoughtful and melancholy. Banda could feel his pity coming: he didn't want it. But what did all this matter now? He instinctively jammed his hand into his pocket and his fingers touched the little packet of bills. Fifteen thousand! He thought; that's real money . . .

"Banda, you should drink something with us, just to forget your woes. Haven't I always said that it was better during our grandfathers' time? They didn't have this kind of trouble. Come and have a drink . . . follow me, brother."

"I'll come, but I won't stay long: my mother's sick."

He wondered how long he'd been in his friend's hut, drinking, dozing, surrounded by all those voices, those laughs. He no longer knew how long he'd been there. He saw the light fading fast. I should have left already, he thought. But he couldn't bring himself to leave. He knew all these boys and girls around him; he didn't like them, but he didn't hate them either. He was constantly on the lookout and outside the conversation. From time to time, he wondered when he was going to leave. Outside, night was falling; the sun, a bright blood red and brilliant ball, was going down behind the trees. He couldn't bring himself to go. He seemed strangely absent. He thought that bad things happen for a reason. If he hadn't run into that young girl, Odilia . . . If Koumé hadn't taken the money from the White man . . . If his cacao hadn't been thrown into the fire, he would never have gotten so much money. He once again did the mental calculation that he had already done innumerable times before: two hundred multiplied by sixty is equal to twelve thousand. All in all he would have gotten twelve thousand francs. Nothing but twelve thousand! And that is assuming that the Greek actually bought his cacao at sixty francs; what if he hadn't kept his word? That happens all the time. You never know with their scales; he might have trimmed off ten or so kilos. Whereas fifteen thousand francs . . . Now, that was real money.

How would his mother react? She'd tell him to take the money to Koumé's parents or to give it to Odilia! Well, he wouldn't say anything about it; it was that simple. He would make up a story to explain the money; any old story as long as he kept it.

To tell the truth, the decision to take possession of the bills dated back to the night before when he had been under the concrete bridge. But while he hadn't thought about it much then, hadn't asked any questions, the more he thought about this appropriation, the more it became difficult to accept. Was he stealing from someone? He had asked himself this many times and had answered in the negative: No, I'm not stealing from anybody. And then the image of Odilia appeared in his mind and stuck: "Come on, he said, after all, Odilia is a woman. She doesn't need money to get married, whereas I . . . And besides, didn't I spontaneously accept to save her brother? I deserve a little reward, right?" But he still wasn't satisfied.

In reality, two voices were speaking in him. One was loud and came up with categorical assertions. It said: "You are doing wrong. This money doesn't belong to you. If you keep it, you are stealing. Give to Caesar what is Caesar's . . ." But Banda wasn't listening to this voice; he didn't want to hear it. First off, according to this voice, the best option would have been to return the money to the widow T. . . . which was quite simply unthinkable. And then because he recognized this voice: it was the missionaries' . . . and also the voice of his mother, who believed in the missionaries. No, under no circumstances would he listen to that voice. He had no doubt what they were about. Ah! They could hold their breath, they wouldn't con him again. Besides, he had never been under their control. He congratulated himself on this.

The other more discrete but also more insistent voice said to him: "Banda, aren't you ashamed? In order to get married, must you steal from a dead man? That boy, when he was alive, was tough, and while he was alive you could never have taken his money like this. He was a real tough, whereas you rob dead bodies. Hah! Aren't you ashamed? Koumé wasn't afraid of that shotgun when he was taking this money—not to mention that he had been working and had fought. He wasn't afraid of Mrs. T.'s shotgun. He was a tough guy . . . And instead of following his example, you plunder his corpse. And what about your idea, your grand idea? Taking only ten thousand francs from a Greek, just enough to get married . . . only ten thousand. So, you're not thinking of your idea anymore? . . . You're not thinking of that anymore, huh? Could Tonga be right? Are you in fact a good-for-nothing, a nobody with grand illusions? Have you been cursed? And why do you want to go to the city? The city only accepts toughs, real tough guys, like Koumé. Wimps like you get rejected, you know? And it's not only Tanga—all cities are like that. To succeed in the city you have to be a tough and not a little girl. Bah . . . Banda, you are robbing the dead, bah! . . . Banda, the good-for-nothing. The zero . . ."

He also recognized this voice: he listened to the inflections, the modulations, all the detours of this voice. He couldn't help loving it, for it was . . . his own voice, as if there were two Bandas . . . He nevertheless tried to quiet this voice by answering it loudly. He said, "And my mother, my poor mother, my mother who has spent her whole life loving me, I can't just let her be miserable 'til the day she dies . . . She would be so happy if I got married. I did what I could. Is it my fault if they put my cacao in the fire? I can't let my mother suffer 'til the day she dies. I'd like to give her a little joy, just a little, before she dies . . ." But the inexorable voice kept repeating: "What a good-for-nothing that Banda is! He's never done anything on his own. He always has to leech off of others . . ." He was extremely unhappy.

He thought of Odilia with bitterness, as if she had been the cause of that voice. Still, he couldn't bring himself to hate the young girl; on the contrary . . . He couldn't say exactly what he felt in thinking of her; he felt that he would like to see her often, to live under the same roof . . . It was very hard to explain; in fact, he didn't push the thought any further.

More and more was being said around him. It was lucky that they were all a little drunk, otherwise they would have wound up figuring out that something was wrong with him. He kept saying to himself that he should be gone by now and kept finding it impossible to leave. He put his hand on his pocket and felt the packet of bills.

Without thinking any more about those around him than if they hadn't existed, he began daydreaming again.

From time to time, he could hear bits and pieces of their conversation. In a burst of laughter, a girl alluded to the fat White man, Mr. T. who died last night at the hospital after having been beaten by his mechanics. Hearing this, Banda, jumped. He just as quickly reproached himself for almost giving himself away: he had to be careful. And perhaps he should stop drinking—it prevented him from controlling himself. But it didn't appear that the story the girl was telling particularly interested the audience; they couldn't have been unaware of the event; ignoring this particular bit of news, they found another topic. Their conversation

once again became harmless. Banda sank back into his daydreaming.

A cloud of red dust was now floating over the road. The
passing car triggered the following exchange, which Banda
picked up by accident:

"What's that big car? Didn't you see it? It's carrying two
White people, a man and his wife. They haven't stopped
traveling up and down the road since this morning. It's
odd . . ."

"Why is it odd? Doesn't the road belong to them? What
do you care if they come or go?"

"Those White people are Greeks. They passed by yesterday morning. I heard they were headed to Douma, you
know, in the South: they have a store there. Yes, and last
night they lost a little suitcase on the road: it's very important to them. That's why they're rushing around."

"What I wonder is how he could lose a little suitcase in
a car like that."

"Perhaps he tied it to the roof rack; he said it was small;
so it could have slipped out on some sharp turn without
him realizing it."

"Heh heh heh . . . He doesn't stop. He just keeps getting
out, getting back in, all for a little suitcase."

"Those are odd people. They never think they have
enough money; they have to keep on making more. Look at
that Greek: he has shops in Tanga, shops in Douma, shops
here, shops there. All in all, he has perhaps ten stores . . .
Millions in profits a month . . . But he would die just for a
little suitcase."

"They aren't the same as we are. As long as we eat,
sleep, have our wives next to us, and are in good health, all
is well . . ."

"And what is life if not those things?"

Banda wasn't listening to them anymore; in fact he
hadn't made any effort to listen to them. The words had just
slipped into his ear of their own accord, despite himself. He
would be surprised, some time later, to remember this conversation, despite having made no effort to listen.

He was tired and hungry: these two sensations suddenly came back to the surface, no doubt made more acute by the palm wine. He rose and took his leave, with an absent expression.

On the road it was hot, and it was already dark because of the bordering palm trees whose branches intertwined over the roadbed. The dust floating in the air smelled heavily of hot, humid, laterite.

As he walked along, he thought to himself that his village was close at hand now and that he wouldn't have to walk much longer: he congratulated himself on that fact.

At the end of the day, I won't go live in Fort-Nègre or even in Tanga, he thought to himself.

Why did that idea suddenly pop into his head? He couldn't have answered. It's just that that voice, that insistent voice, had made him lose all confidence in himself. Ever since it had begun crying out, "Banda, you good-for-nothing," he had started thinking of himself as useless. What was most important to him was to make his mother happy, to get married so as to provide her with some small joy before she died. For once, she'd be happy. He wanted her to have this pleasure just once, even if he had to pay with the conviction that he would always be a deluded zero, a good-for-nothing.

He really believed this the moment when, braving this voice, his own voice, he had opted to take the money. Was he a zero? It didn't matter as long as his mother was happy just once in her life. And nothing would make her happier than seeing him get married. Pride had given way to filial love or rather filial pity. He really did believe that he was a good-for-nothing living under the crush of a terrible curse.

The rapidly falling night soothed him. He dreamed of Odilia. He told himself that, had he had a sister, he would have felt the same way in seeing her. Always this same sensation of kinship!

And all of a sudden he stopped. Why had he not thought of it earlier? . . . Damn! Why, of course, wasn't ten thousand francs almost enough for his marriage? That's what

he would do. He would give five thousand francs to Odilia as if that were all the money he had found in Koumé's
pocket. Wouldn't that be a way of betraying himself? He
had to be careful. Would she believe him? Of course she
would; five thousand francs is already a lot. How much did
her brother earn a month? A thousand eight hundred, two
thousand francs maybe; in any case, not more. He couldn't
have earned more that two thousand francs a month. Five
thousand francs is already a lot, by God! She would believe
him. Of course she would believe him . . .

He breathed deeply. He swallowed. Life wasn't so bad
after all. Was it really that bad? In the falling light, he felt a
melancholy desire to speak, to share secrets, to make friends
with all the vegetation, running along both sides of the
road. Up until that day, life had felt like an endless morning rain, cold and dark. And suddenly, even though it was
almost dark, the whole earth was taken over by an abundant daybreak that brought with it the promise of abundant
sunshine on the horizon. The birds were singing at the top
of their lungs and the brook babbled more gaily than ever.

He wanted to leave the road and climb up on the narrow sidewalk in order to get rid of the palm wine that was
weighing on his belly. But, in lifting his foot, he caused a
few pebbles to roll down the embankment. These, arriving
at the streambed, made an unexpected metallic sound. Nevertheless, he first relieved himself. It's only afterward that
he sent a few more stones rolling down the embankment:
the metallic sound was confirmed. Having climbed down
into the streambed, he discovered that the stones were simply falling against the famous suitcase, the Greek's suitcase.
There was no doubt; that was the suitcase, the one he had
heard described. There could be no mistake.

Wow! The Greek had promised a substantial reward for
it . . . That's what they had just mentioned in his friend's
cabin. But did they really say that or did he imagine it? Huh,
did they really say it? Yes, I know they did. He even remembered the boy who had said it. Addressing someone else, he
had spoken in the following manner:

"If you want to, go help him find his suitcase, he promised a substantial reward to whoever would help him find it . . ."

"I'd rather prevent him from getting it, because if he wants it that badly, God only knows what it contains . . ."

Yeah! He remembered that and yet he hadn't listened to them. Still, he had heard it. No, he wasn't dreaming. He could even name the boy . . .

12

LITTLE BY LITTLE, the young girl realized that Banda's mother was not in fact as old as she at first appeared. The disease had made her dry and leathery and had prematurely aged her. Odilia felt sorry for her.

Soon after Banda's departure, and Tonga's, which followed shortly thereafter, the two women lying face to face on either side of the fire had fallen asleep without exchanging a word. The next day, Sunday, Odilia arose early out of habit. She washed, which consisted in rubbing her face, her arms, and her legs with cool water. She then rejoined the sick woman.

"Do you need something?" she asked.

Banda's mother raised her eyes to the young girl; she considered her for a long moment and responded:

"My, what a good heart you have, little girl! But my God you slept well last night . . . I listened to the rhythm of your breathing, which was quiet and regular, and it did me good to hear you sleep. I felt as if I were the one sleeping."

Without telling her if she needed anything, she advised Odilia as to what she should do, where she should go when she was hungry.

She immediately surprised Odilia with her penchant for jokes, which she was the first to laugh at; she told them regularly. She also hummed songs that were inevitably about a young girl lamenting a man who had abandoned her. The girl in the song spoke to him despite the distance; she said that she awaited him; she asked him to hurry; but the lover still did not return. It's odd, the sick woman herself commented, they never come back. Odilia understood that in all of this the sick woman found something akin to her own tragedy, and she felt even more sorry for her. But at the same time, the young girl wondered if perhaps this woman was not so sick that she would die? She had seen many sick people about to die; they didn't have this vitality. Perhaps in caring for her well, Odilia would succeed in healing her?

"Do you occasionally get out of bed?" Odilia asked innocently, and just as quickly she regretted her naiveté; she should instead have told her to signal whenever she felt like getting up.

"Of course I sometimes get out of bed." She laughed softly. "For example, I'm going to help you prepare our meal."

Soon after, Sabina, Regina, and all the women who usually nursed the patient came in one after the other. Their faces brightened in turn at the sight of Odilia as they admired her beauty and youth while making sure not to make the slightest remark. But, though they held their tongues, you could tell they'd all been taken with her. They didn't stay long. They each took their leave while joking lightly. If a replacement had been found for them, they hadn't asked for it, but as long there was one, they would leave, even if it meant returning that evening.

It was progressively, with some difficulty, and with infinite care on both sides, that the two women had opened up to one another. Odilia noted the long—not necessarily hostile, but rather, slightly questioning—look to which Banda's mother had subjected her: one might have thought she was weighing, evaluating. She was happy that she was examining her like this. If their eyes met, the sick woman lowered hers first, with a shyness and modesty that made the young girl slightly uncomfortable.

The time came when the two women slowly began to share their thoughts. The sick woman had returned to bed, saying that she felt dizzy when she was sitting up. She began. She spoke of her son who would soon be alone—she said this in the same tone she might have used with a neighbor with whom she felt at ease. Her son would never make it. With his violent temperament, he made many enemies and few friends. More than anything, he didn't have much luck. No, he had very little luck. It's true that he had never had any religious sentiments at all. Still, she knew others who had Banda's disposition and who did very well in life. Her son imagined that muscles could solve everything. His solitude was topmost in her mind. She gazed off into the distance and sighed deeply as she spoke of it. How sad! At his age he still wasn't married, while the son of so-and-so who was two years younger had a wife now and even a child.

Odilia wondered at how such a seemingly proud woman could address the problem so directly. She was unaware of the kind of defensive strategy that was Banda's mother's mechanical approach to city women—which Odilia was in the woman's eyes. Still, she finally realized that there was no ulterior motive, no suggestion in what the woman was saying, a fact that came as a disagreeable surprise.

One would have been hard pressed to find any hint of complaint in the sick woman's single-minded voice. There were no tears in her eyes. She looked so absent that she appeared to already belong to another world. She wasn't worried about her approaching death. Wasn't she right with God? Besides, what evil had she ever done? She had stayed faithful to her husband, after having served him while he was alive. She had brought up her son. She had wanted to make a Christian of him. Was it her fault if she hadn't succeeded? She had assisted those she could help, giving food to those who were hungry and water to those who were thirsty. Her whole life, she had done nothing but work. Then she got sick just like that, one night, upon returning from the fields. She lay down and was not able to get up the next morning. She thought at first it would be a passing problem, but it wasn't. The disease had permanently occupied her flesh. Periods of moderate health had alternated with bouts of severe illness. And then one day, a few months back, she had become permanently bed-ridden.

She talked at length about everything her son had done in the hope of healing her. He brought vast quantities of little white, yellow, red, or black seeds that one had to chew or swallow with water. He took her to the clinic at least six times. She had even been hospitalized for weeks, but she had to leave when her son's money ran out. And, naturally, all that was to no avail. Besides, her health didn't matter. If it weren't for her son she would be happy to die, to die soon. Wasn't she going to be reunited with her husband and all those who died before her? But what would they tell her? she wondered.

"What makes you think you are going to die so soon?" Odilia asked.

"Oh, I don't have any illusions about that," she had answered. "You see, little girl, when you've been a woman like me, who worked and everything, who has been strong, and you fall to where I am today, you realize what's going on. No, I'm done, there's no doubt about it."

She stayed silent and pensive for a long time, her mouth open, eyes shining; her gaze remained distant, as if surprised, but resigned in advance. Finally, she declared:

"Life, what a strange thing!"

What particularly struck Odilia was the contrast between the pathetic physique of this human wreck and the dignity of what she said: she couldn't help but admire Banda's mother. She wondered what she must have been like in her youth. The young man must have inherited his impetuous and generous personality from his mother. She must have mulled over an awful lot as she lay there like that. As a result, the young girl forgot about her own misfortune, her dead brother, the sadness that brought her to a point where she almost thought she would choke.

When she thought of Koumé, she made an immediate connection between the two young men—Koumé inevitably evoked Banda. It seemed to her that they had been created to meet each other one day, to help each other, to advance shoulder to shoulder across the inextricable jumble of life. What a tragedy that one of them should die! Perhaps she would have done better yesterday to tell Koumé her dream. He would have made fun of it, but he might have been moved. Instead, she had argued with him.

She could again see him with his elbows resting against the windowsill, calling out suggestive comments to the passing women. "I know how to handle dust-ups with bastards like T. . . ."—that's the last thing he said, yesterday morning. And this had only just happened yesterday. She would never see him again, never again. Yes, on the other side . . .

At the same time, Banda's image, the very sound of his name, his whole appearance, which she could recall with surprising precision, seemed familiar, as if she had known him for years, forever. She couldn't convince herself that she had only just met him last night . . . Was that even possible?

"Little girl, what's your name?"

She was suddenly drawn out of her daydream.

"Odilia! They call me Odilia."

"Odilia, do you feel better, my child?"

She seemed surprised.

"Come now, you were sick last night."

"Ah! Yes," said the young woman, sheepishly, "I feel a lot better now. Not my first headache. It's nothing serious, nothing serious at all."

The silence returned, awkward this time. Odilia felt she owed Banda's mother an explanation. But she didn't dare give it to her. Hadn't the young man very explicitly forbidden her to say anything? Yet, she felt she owed this woman an explanation. At the bottom of her heart she desperately wanted to confide in her, and she could only do that after explaining herself. The sick woman gave her the opportunity by saying:

"Last night your eyes were red and swollen. It looked like you'd been crying."

Odilia rapidly told her everything, without forgetting a single detail. She told her the name of the village where she was born, the name of her tribe, the name of her father, and that she had only been living in Tanga for two or three weeks when last night's events took place. When she got to this point in her story the sick woman appeared to perk up. Her face brightened, expressing a kind of infinite sympathy. Odilia took good note of this change; but she couldn't explain this return of good will. The sick woman was simply losing her initial suspicions because she had first thought she was from the city, with all that implies, and it turned out that she wasn't; as a result of this discovery, a whole vista of hope and deliverance opened in front of Banda's mother. The young woman had finished her story and become quiet.

"You see, daughter," the sick woman said, "who can say what will happen to all these children who abandon their villages and their families and go to the city? In our time, if a White man said, 'Kneel,' you kneeled. Or, 'get on your stomach so I can whip your behind!' and you got down as low as you could to the ground. Today, with our sons, it's not the same anymore. They have grown up, and they scorn us because we bowed down to the Whites. For their part, they walk proudly while beating their chests, while raising their arms, brandishing their fists. The Whites said, 'Why don't you come to our schools?' They went to their schools, they learned to speak their language, how to discuss things with them, to calculate on pieces of paper the way they do. They learned how to operate terrible machines that chop down trees, dig roads; they drive around in trucks at infernal speeds—they do everything the Whites do. The result is that they don't want to be taken for servants anymore, for simple slaves like their fathers. They want to be considered equal to the Whites. And what do the latter think of all this, I wonder? Are they going to relinquish their roles as masters? Or will they refuse this change? In any case, how can we know what will happen? I know that Banda doesn't like Bamila, his father's village, the land of his ancestors. After my death he wants to go to the White people's city like so many others. I disapprove in advance. May the tragedy that he has witnessed serve as a lesson! Oh, my God!"

She dozed off soon thereafter.

When the day began to fade and the sun brushed the treetops shining from the previous day's rain, Odilia went out to sit on the narrow veranda; it was cool at that time of day.

For hours on end, she expected to see Banda appear on the road, from the north or the south, but he didn't appear. She wondered if something had happened to him. He shouldn't be so late. Anxiety was starting to dry her throat.

From time to time, a group of people would walk by on the road. They were generally returning from Tanga, where they had gone to mass. She could hear them talking: she followed their voices until she couldn't hear them anymore. That's how she discovered that her brother's body had been discovered at dawn under the cement bridge. The body, they said, had a deep wound at the back of the head. Someone must have killed him with something like a hammer. They had deposited him under the bridge to make it look like he had fallen, perhaps, or like it was some such sort of accident. Everybody knew that they were the ones who had killed him. Who had they charged with doing this dirty deed? Most likely a territorial guard. The territorial guards had arrived in force last night. After so much searching, they must have finally gotten their hands on him—it wouldn't be the first time something like this had happened. And the Whites had said to them, "Go ahead and kill him; that will teach him to confront White people. We are losing patience with these little children, with their unruly arrogance. This can't go on much longer. Go ahead and kill him. At least that way he won't stand up to any more Whites. Woe unto whoever stands up to a White person! That's what others will say!" And they had killed him! They had really killed him, their brother, such a young boy, almost a child. When you killed a White man, you might as well kill yourself since, no matter what, one could be sure of the final outcome. Koumé should have killed himself—that way they wouldn't have gotten him . . .

But beyond what they brought back indirectly, she could only think of Banda. She eavesdropped in vain, but the young man was never the topic of conversation.

Suddenly, she decided not to think about it any more. Several times she saw the Greek and his wife go by in their big black car, come back and stop. They said they had lost an object on the road the name of which she couldn't quite make out. They would give a very large reward to whoever would help them find it. Each time she only paid vague attention, preoccupied as she was with the imagined dangers threatening Banda. Again, she took the strong resolution to not think about it any more. And perhaps in this way Banda would just spring forth all of a sudden? In truth, it was tough for her to forget the boy she had first discovered in that smoky low-roofed hut that she had never entered before. Come to think of it, why had she gone in there? To find that girlfriend . . . Couldn't she tell that her friend wasn't in there from the door? It seemed to her that it was an outside force, a kind of fate that had pushed her inside.

She tried to turn her mind to the kids who were playing in the dust a few huts over. Still farther away, young men were going in and out of a building, calling out to each other, and laughing without any apparent reason. They were throwing lively comments back and forth to each other, accompanied with grand mocking gestures. They were wearing their wraps nonchalantly around their waists, in a way that was intentionally obscene. Some wore khaki shorts, often patched or falling apart. They seemed to take particular pleasure in stroking their pectoral muscles, in slapping each other on the back. They vaunted their various exploits loudly without the least modesty, punctuating their words with knowing laughter, to the point where you might have thought that in this village, nobody ever cried, that it was endless euphoria. It almost seemed as if they were doing it on purpose to get closer, passing back and forth in front of her, some distance away, while casting reticent glances her way. From their manifest lack of concern, she recognized them as Tonga's people, his toadies: it wasn't surprising that he preferred those guys to Banda!

She caught herself contemplating Bamila, famous, grand, ferocious Bamila.

The night was resolutely falling; it was viscous and hot. Odilia went back into the hut. The sick woman had awoken; she remained prone, drawn up on herself, pensive: that must be her habitual posture.

"Why didn't you tell me you were awake? I wouldn't have left you alone so long . . ."

The young woman spoke with a certain disappointment.

"Daughter, I didn't know where you were; I didn't know . . ."

She said this in such a breezy fashion that Odilia stopped resenting her for it. She asked her, "Do you like being alone?"

"It's not that I like it, little girl, it's that I'm used to it . . ."

"Which means that you like it."

"If you want . . ."

She laughed softly but without ill feelings. Odilia had just become somber again. The sick woman noticed.

"What's wrong with you, my daughter? Has something happened?"

"Banda still hasn't come home," the little girl said, with a pout.

"Don't worry, Odilia, my child, don't worry. He can remain absent for weeks, but he always comes back. A man is not a child or a woman, he doesn't get lost: he always finds his way. When he doesn't come home it's often that he has problems that he doesn't want to talk about. Don't worry—he can stay away for weeks, but he always comes back."

Hey! He had also said that to her with respect to Koumé; he had used the same language. How mother and son resembled each other.

"But yesterday," the girl protested, "he promised to come back today during the daytime. They discovered my brother's body at dawn under the cement bridge, some passersby were just saying it. Why doesn't he return? It's strange."

"He'll come back, it's a sure thing that he'll come back, tonight even, though maybe a little late, but he'll be back, I'm telling you."

Odilia hesitated and then she burst.

"Perhaps something happened to him?"

"Like what?"

"I don't know, any old thing. Do I know?"

"Did you hear something?"

All that this question implied suddenly frightened her.

"No! Nothing at all. I haven't heard anything." She was quiet; then started again: "Maybe I'd better go out onto to the road to see if he isn't on his way. If only I could know which direction he'll come from . . . I wish he were back so much . . ."

The sick woman didn't say a word. From time to time, she gave the young girl a perplexed look and just as quickly turned away. Odilia herself was surprised to have said so much; yet, what she most wanted to express remained unsaid; she was unable to bring herself to voice it. She made a final effort:

"Tell me," she began after a long pause. "What is Banda going to do now? What is he planning? He has no money and yet he wants to marry that girl. What is he planning to do?"

"My God! Daughter, I also wonder that, I do. I would give anything to know."

The gloom was filling the hut and the fire barely lit it, while producing a constant ebb and flow of shadows. Odilia sat facing the sick woman, looking at her fixedly. Her whole being expressed an extreme aggressiveness: her ardent gaze flashed, her eyelids fluttered; she panted, her lips were tight. When the eyes of the sick woman met hers, Odilia put on an air of absolute indifference.

"It seemed to me," she said in a soft voice, "it seemed to me that when one can't marry one woman, well, one marries another. Why not? For example, he could go get married in a place where he wouldn't have to pay a bride-price . . . You know, where I come from, they no longer talk about money when you get married. One pays nothing, not a cent. A few years ago those in my country came together and decided this . . ."

The sick woman seemed not to understand. With a willfulness that came close to heroism, Odilia continued:

"It's true. Where I come from, when a young man wants to marry a girl, he doesn't have to give his father-in-law money beforehand. That's true, believe me . . . Your son should come to my country. He would certainly find a girl he likes. He would be welcome. He is so kind, so likeable . . . Girls don't refuse boys like him."

She was quiet. On the road a car passed by slowly; the two women recognized it because of its incessant honking—it was at least the hundredth time that it had passed by. They commented on the Greeks. Deep down, they were grateful to the driver for distracting them for a moment, giving them the opportunity to catch their breath. Still, the atmosphere remained heavy and tense. They stayed silent. They were both waiting for something; they appeared to be eyeing each other. And all of a sudden Banda's mother lanced the boil:

"Would you agree to marry my son?" she bluntly asked the young girl.

This question caused Odilia to jump. How lucid this woman was! She was filled with a sense of infinite gratitude, because she had made the task easier by helping her say what she might never have been able to admit on her own. She was suddenly relieved. She would have a brother, another brother who equaled the first in every imaginable way.

"Me . . . Ahhh! How would I know? Does one ask that kind of question? Is there is a girl in the world who wouldn't want a boy like Banda? He has such a big heart, and he's so dedicated and courageous . . ."

And then suddenly she burst into tears that she couldn't contain, that shook her to the core. The sick woman believed she was crying at the memory of her brother; this had already happened several times this morning.

"You know Odilia, I sympathize with your pain," she said by way of consolation, while a tear hung on the young girl's cheek.

"Yesterday, it was my brother," the young girl stuttered. "Will I never have any luck? What could have happened to him?"

"To whom?"

"Well, to Banda of course!"

At that moment, someone pushed open the wooden door with authority and entered the hut. It was Banda. He was carrying a little suitcase in his hand. Odilia quickly wiped her eyes.

"My word!" he said, "you must've cried all day. Calm down, you're going to make yourself sick."

Like his mother, he thought she was crying at the thought of her brother.

13

IN TAKING THE SUITCASE from the bottom of the streambed, Banda had realized that he now possessed three secrets: the first, Koumé's death, he shared with the young girl; the second, the secret of Koumé's money, he held alone; the third, the secret of the Greek's suitcase. It had seemed to him that he would suffocate under the weight of this knowledge if he had to hold on to it for too long. Thankfully, in a few hundred meters, he would enter Bamila: that was a relief.

He felt stiff. He didn't want to show himself. People would ask questions about the controllers and his dispute with the regional guards and about the suitcase. He hated certain people's questions. He decided to walk behind the huts, quietly skirting the walls. He was thankful for the night's readiness to help him by hiding him from indiscrete gazes: he felt as if he were rediscovering a familiar ally— the night was now and forever a friend and accomplice. He remembered all the highs and lows of his adventure, last night, on the river, with Koumé's body. To tell the truth, he thought proudly, nobody can argue that I'm a good-for-nothing.

He immediately thought of the Greek whose suitcase he had just found. He'd promised a substantial reward? How much would he give? Perhaps ten thousand? No, that was too much, that number was perhaps too high. But what was ten thousand francs to him? Nothing at all. With his millions in profits a month, ten thousand francs was nothing. Maybe the Greek would give him ten thousand francs . . . Yeah! Ten thousand was exactly what he needed. If he gave him ten thousand, he would abandon the idea of pulling something off on a Greek, he'd have gotten what he was after. Yes, the Greek would give him the ten thousand francs, and it would be as if he had actually pulled something off. Ten thousand! More or less what he would have gotten for his cacao. Life is strange.

Pushing open the door to the hut, he knew exactly what he would do. Though he still wasn't certain of getting ten thousand francs from the Greek, he knew that he would give Odilia all the money he'd found on her brother; it was clear and simple; he would return that. As soon as he had made this decision, he had immediately regained his self-confidence, and with it the conviction that he would go to Fort-Nègre. The voice no longer said to him: "Banda, you'll never be anything but a good-for-nothing, nothing but a zero with big ideas . . . The Banda that I love! Hey, you are right to be proud of yourself . . . And now you can go to Fort-Nègre, after the death of your mother. You've earned it . . ." Would the Greek really give him ten thousand francs?

Perhaps he'd do well to wait and see if the Greek actually gave him ten thousand francs . . . No! He would wait for nothing. He would give the young girl the money immediately. He shouldn't wait. Why wouldn't the Greek give him ten thousand francs? What was ten thousand to him? Nothing at all.

The idea that he was going to make things right by the young girl gave him a joy that surprised him in its intensity. As long as he was convinced that he was appropriating it, that money seemed to erect a wall between them, but now, with increasing pleasure, he sensed how the young girl was becoming more important to him. How long would she agree to continue to stay with them? If only he knew. Perhaps he'd accompany her home just to protect her. And perhaps the Greek would give him ten thousand francs . . .

Yeah! More or less what his cacao would have earned him
. . . He would be the one to accompany the young girl to her
home, just to protect her. One never knows. He hoped she
didn't want to leave tomorrow morning. There was some
degree of doubt, he must have seen that girl somewhere.
But where? Her village was far away, and she had only been
living in Tanga for a few weeks. And before yesterday, he
hadn't set foot in Tanga for over a month . . . Where could he
have seen her before? Perhaps several times in his dreams.
How long would she stay with them? He would accompany
her home to protect her—the country wasn't safe.

He was very surprised to find the young girl on the bed,
facing his mother, in exactly the same place and position as
he had left her the night before.

"Mother," he begged, "Mother, didn't you keep her from
crying? She has stayed seated on that same bed at that same
spot since last night, isn't that right, Mother? She has done
nothing but cry all day and you did nothing to stop it? You
should have prevented her from crying like this . . ."

Odilia herself was the one to protest in a firm and un-
wavering voice: no one would have thought that she had
just been crying her heart out. She hadn't remained seated
on the bed in the same spot since last night. No, last night
she had slept until late in the morning. She hadn't spent the
whole time crying. No, she had done numerous chores.

"In fact, I'm going to serve you the meal I prepared."

She had spoken with an affected volubility that for that
same reason was painful, all the more so in that he knew
she'd been crying. He remained standing in the middle of
the hut and looked at her coming and going. He was certain that he'd seen her before going into that dive. He was
positive.

It seemed to him that the young girl was avoiding his
gaze. Luckily, he thought, I'm going to give her all her money. He was worried.

The sick woman stoked the fire. A small flame appeared, grew, and began to sway like a little girl moving to

the sound of a xylophone. At the same time, the hut was teeming with shadows that shook: the spectacle evoked a multitude of dancers gyrating in the moonlight.

He stayed there, standing, with his suitcase hanging from his arm, confused by his dreams, his desires, his fears.

"Son, what's that suitcase?" the sick woman asked.

"He should eat first," the young woman advised. "He'll tell us in due course."

He wondered if they had spoken much, and if they had gotten along, what they possibly could have said to each other. He soon realized that Odilia was as comfortable with his mother as if she had lived in the house for months; that made him happy. Perhaps she would agree to spend another week with them, just a little week. Why not? She would wind up returning to her country, to her parents who would have only suffered a few days of anxiety. He really wanted Odilia to spend a few more days with them. He couldn't imagine what would happen at the end of this stay; to be frank, he didn't want to imagine it. For now, his whole being was focused on getting her to stay a little longer. He had no clear intention: he simply wanted to see the young girl a little longer.

He finally sat down on the bed facing his mother, next to Odilia. Their bodies brushed up against each other ever so lightly; she moved away imperceptibly—or so he thought. In reality, it didn't escape Banda's notice: he was deeply disappointed. Was she mad at him for something? Why was she mad? Her behavior had changed since the night in that dive . . . That night she had let him touch her; she had abandoned her hand to him . . . Perhaps tonight she wouldn't let him take her hand? He was going to take her hand just to see. Yes, he was going to try to take her hand just to see . . . But all of a sudden, he realized that his mother and she were staring at him. With the hand that was already preparing the gesture he instead wiped his face and rubbed his eyes:

"Ah," he sighed, "I'm so tired! I don't know what I'm doing anymore . . ."

They looked at him with astonished and admiring expressions. At least, the mother thought, I won't have given birth to a slave, a weakling, but a man, a real one and not an imitation. My God, the young girl said to herself, he looks exactly like my poor brother. He's actually smarter and more thoughtful. His penchant for devotion and generosity . . . Perhaps it's being around his sick mother that has led him to pity those in misery . . . But it's odd how unlucky he is! True, my brother was also unlucky . . .

Like a little girl at the sound of the xylophone, the flame danced: it jumped, pranced, gathered itself, and pounced, and in the same rhythm the shadows on the walls did a mad jig.

While he ate, he dreamed of the Greek, Demetropoulos . . . His name was Demetropoulos—it was a funny name. What would this Demetropoulos give him? He would have so liked to know. What could he possibly give him? Perhaps ten thousand, just ten thousand . . . Would he first congratulate him before giving him the reward? Would he first speak to him in flattering and agreeable tones? Or would he simply give him the reward without congratulating him? He couldn't care less about praise. All he wanted was Demetropoulos's money: he was asking for nothing besides his money, not even agreeable words. Good boy . . . Most excellent boy . . . He wasn't interested in all that.

He knew this Demetropoulos well. He knew him all too well. And he didn't like him, not even a bit. It's true that he wasn't exactly attractive: his nose was too big and was shaped like an eagle's beak, his belly was getting fat, he had fake teeth; he really wasn't too attractive.

He couldn't like this Demetropoulos. One day, he had seen him do something terrible, something horrible. It was during the cacao season, a few years back. Demetropoulos was set up in front of his shop and wanted to buy cacao. He waited, leaning against his steelyard, surrounded by his men, who called out in vain. The peasants passed by, taking their cacao with them, without even casting a glance at

Demetropoulos. So that bastard hatched a diabolic plan. He asked someone next to him to bring him some small coins, pieces of scented soap, knives, bottles of perfume, combs, piles of cheap junk. He began digging into this mound of objects and throwing them into the street, just like that. The peasants couldn't resist; they came running and dove down. Banda remembered seeing men fight over a knife or a harmonica; he had seen children roll around on the ground in a tight embrace for a coin and emerge bloodied. He had seen women scratch each other, bite each other, rip each other's clothes for a comb or a bottle of perfume. All the while, Demetropoulos was laughing and slapping his thigh. Why had he done that? No, he could never like this Demetropoulos. And he had stores all across the country. And it was said that ten years earlier, he had come from his country to Fort-Nègre with nothing. At the time, all he had to his name was a poor cardboard suitcase, canvas shoes; nothing but what he had been wearing when coming off the boat. And today he had trucks, big cars, and even a wife, a beautiful wife, who perhaps even came from his own country—they spoke an incomprehensible language between themselves. He often saw this woman with her elbows on the windowsill but never in the street.

That Demetropoulos! If he had stuck to his idea of trying to pull something off on a Greek it sure would have been Demetropoulos. Yeah. All he wanted was the reward; he didn't want flowery speech. And he would even refuse the reward if it weren't for his mother . . . He would keep the suitcase, or, since he wouldn't be able to open it, he would go and throw it into the middle of the river. Just so Demetropoulos would never find it.

He had to be careful when he went to the city. He would have to watch out or he would start something worse than what Koumé had done. He would be careful, otherwise he would simply and purely kill a White man like Demetropoulos or Mr. T. He didn't like evil people. The desire to punish them would be so strong that he'd fall for it. He'd have to be very careful. If a White man like Mr. T. or Demetropoulos hit him, he would hold his arms down by his side: he'd lower his eyes so as not to see those of his adversary, otherwise he would not be able to resist the temptation to kill him, to strangle him, to pummel him with blows until he died. But what would happen to him then?

By the way, was this really his little suitcase? He examined the small box closely. What could it possibly contain? He had, of course, already tried unsuccessfully to open it. It corresponded to what he had heard described by accident and remembered.

He finished eating. He knew that he was the object of the two silent women's intense curiosity. With slow movements, with an exaggerated look of fatigue, he put his hand down into the left pocket of his khaki shorts. He took the little packet of bills that he slowly undid. He lit a cigarette that he inhaled hungrily. He was surprised to find himself attaching so little importance to this money now. He counted out the bills into the palm of the stunned young woman. Only afterward did he explain everything to her. Hearing her brother's name, she burst into tears.

"Please don't cry, little sister," he whispered into her ear.

In reality, he wasn't unhappy that she should begin to cry. He thought that if she cried, he could pretend to console her and thereby take her hand, or caress her hair, once again repeating all the gestures whose memory made her so tender and loveable. But she stopped crying, and he didn't dare take her hand. Perhaps she wouldn't like it anymore?

He caught sight of the black pupil, the absent air of the sick woman who was looking fixedly at the flame. He said to her, "Mother, do you see this suitcase, this little thing? I'm told this belongs to a Greek. I wonder how it could have fallen from his car while he was returning from God knows where."

"That's the suitcase?" the young woman exclaimed, her eyes wide, her mouth round.

He became frightened. Had the real suitcase already been found?

"I don't know. Why?"

"No! I was just asking . . ."

"I don't know. It just seemed to me that it answered the description."

No, the true suitcase had not yet been found. He breathed more freely. He told the story of how he had found it. They answered that they had heard about this suitcase and that the Greek had promised a large reward. I didn't dream it then, Banda thought. I didn't dream: in other words, he did promise a reward, a large reward. How much would he give? Maybe ten thousand francs . . . Why not? They also told him that the Greek kept driving along the road, back and forth. He would stop in each village, and they waited to see if someone had found the suitcase. He had just passed going south, and he would pass through again soon. That's all he had done all day long. His wife was at his side, she hadn't left him since this morning. She was by his side in their large black car. It was odd. She who never left the house, she who nobody ever saw except at the window, never in the street . . . She hadn't left his side since this morning.

"They say," Odilia remarked, "that the suitcase is filled with things that belong to her, that are very valuable."

"What could it be?" the sick woman asked.

All three looked at the little box with curiosity.

"I too," Banda said, "I too would like to know what's in there. I tried to open it, but I could spend a year trying and I don't believe I'd succeed."

"If it's true that the suitcase contains objects that belong to her, very valuable ones," the young girl said, "then they must be rings, or gold bracelets, or very expensive necklaces."

"You think so?" Banda responded, skeptical.

"What else could it be?" Odilia said impatiently.

"I don't know," said Banda. "I'd love to know. Very valuable objects belonging to a young White woman. What could it be, I wonder? It could be anything . . ."

"It's gold rings, bracelets, necklaces, earrings . . ."

"What would she do with that stuff in Tanga? Little sister, I ask you? What do you want her to do with it in Tanga?

She never goes out into the street. The necklaces, the rings, the gold bracelets, all that is for women who go out to big parties to dance, or simply to show themselves off and to be admired: that's for the wives of the Frenchmen. But a Greek woman . . . When two Greeks meet, it's only to talk about business. I know them. And in fact, that one, Mrs. Demetropoulos, she never goes out any farther than her veranda. I would love to know what she has in her suitcase . . ."

"Don't worry yourselves over it, my children," the sick woman said, laughing. "If someone opened this suitcase for you, you might be surprised and disappointed. Perhaps it contains something totally unimportant . . ."

"Photographs of her parents," Odilia suggested, her face brightening all of a sudden.

"Or love letters," Banda said.

Neither of the two women seemed to understand what importance love letters might have for a White woman. Banda was disappointed by this and didn't insist.

"Or things that had belonged to her parents," Odilia proposed.

"Oh! Yes, that's very possible," the sick woman approved.

"It could be any old thing, simple objects of that sort," the young woman said.

"Or surprising objects," Banda ventured, coming to Odilia's rescue, "for example hair from a woman or human bones . . ."

"Bones?" the sick woman exclaimed, sticking out her tongue in horror. "Son, did you say human bones?"

"Sure, Mother. Those people are astonishing. For example, didn't you know that all of the Catholic churches hold human bones somewhere, often at the altar? The bone of a saint . . . They love souvenirs of that sort. For them, nothing beats a bone or hair as a way of remembering someone. Mother, you wouldn't believe it: they are strange people.

"Are you sure of what you're saying, son? A human bone!"

"Yes, Mother, a human bone . . ."

"In the church!"

"A saint's bone, a 'relic' as they say."

"And what is this bone for?"

"Oh, not much. From time to time they take it out and expose it. At such times, everybody comes to look at it, simply contemplate it. On rare occasions, they touch it."

"Son," she concluded, "you know a great deal about religion, and much more than I."

"Haven't I always said so, Mother?"

"So why aren't you a believer, then?"

"Precisely because I know so much about their religion. That's why I can't believe: I don't trust them."

"How so?"

"It's too hard to explain, Mother. Let's not speak of it anymore, ok?"

"Son, in the beginning you didn't know that much about it. Why didn't you go to catechism when you were thirteen or fourteen?"

"I don't know, Mother. Please, let's not talk about it any more . . ."

All three were quiet. It would have been difficult to guess what the two women were dreaming about. Banda, for his part, was moved by his mother's last question. It had been a long time since she'd asked him about religion. Why was she doing so tonight with the same insistence as she used to show in the past? The whiff of a premonition wafted over him.

Suddenly, his thoughts came back to the bag. He wondered if it really contained a precious object. He would have liked to know what pleasure, what great pleasure it would give Demetropoulos. In the young man's mind, the size of the reward would be proportionate to Demetropoulos's pleasure. But what's precious to a White man? Money? Certainly, since they spend their whole lives running after money, even when they have hoarded enough to fill the church in Tanga. Yet, a White man would also kill you over some seemingly meaningless thing, a photograph, a book, something pitiable. And just as suddenly, he gave up thinking about it.

"Listen to me, son," the sick woman said, breaking the silence. "Listen to me for a moment, only for a moment."

"Of course, Mother, I'm listening," he answered in a tired voice.

"Take a good look at that young woman next to you. Go ahead."

Startled, he glanced at Odilia, who was gazing away from him; he slowly turned back to his mother.

"No, really take a good look at her," his mother said impatiently.

"Well! Mother? I know her, and much better than you. What are you trying to say?"

Perhaps because she was bedridden, perhaps due to the constant suffering of her body and her heart, perhaps from constantly brooding over things, she had finally gone crazy.

"What are you trying to say, mother?"

"Will you marry her?"

"Who?"

"That young girl next to you? Tell me that you'll marry her. You will, right?"

"But Mother, how should I know? I'll try. What if she won't have me?"

"And what if she did want you as her husband!"

"Well in that case, mother, I'd marry her, since that is what you want."

After a moment of silence, the sick woman said, "I'll have waited my whole life for you to find her. And now it's happened: she's an angel sent by God, a real one. I can leave now. I'll announce a joyous event to your father when I get to the other side."

And all of sudden it seemed to the young man that he was being awoken from a long and painful nightmare. Wed Odilia! He hadn't thought of it for an instant, despite the room she had come to occupy in his mind since her first appearance in that dive, when she'd sat down next to him as if guided by fate. Since yesterday evening, he'd lived in a world that was his, exclusively. Without knowing it, he had been fighting artificial enemies.

It's simply that marrying that girl for whom so much money was being asked had become an obsession, a challenge that his ego demanded that he win at all cost. It's true that at the beginning, the desire to provide his poor mother with one little glimmer of happiness had been the real reason for his decision. But little by little, another reason had taken over; that had occurred after he'd met his fiancée.

The young girl hadn't seemed to displease the sick woman who had rejected so many before her. Perhaps the mother had refrained from speaking her mind simply because she didn't want to discourage her son. In any case, she had not *in limine* apposed her usual veto. From that moment on, Banda had sworn to marry that woman whom his mother didn't dislike, even though he didn't feel anything particular for her, besides a certain physical attraction, perhaps. It was mostly a matter of providing a last joy to the poor woman who had so loved him and who was irrevocably condemned to die soon—at least that is what she said and believed. But little by little, as the obstacles began to accumulate, Banda had clung to his enterprise with a desperate obstinacy, more, now, to affirm himself than for any other reason: there come times, most often dramatic, when one feels the pressing need to test one's high opinion of oneself. At such moments, a failure can put everything into question; even more painfully, it can force the subject into a cycle of self-doubt that revises the person's entire conception of the world, prompting him to turn his back on the man he has been to that point. Banda preferred the most self-assuring success; that's why he had stuck to his project.

He had thus armed himself with all the patience he had at his disposal. He had accumulated the money, coin by coin. Adding the sale of his two hundred kilos of cacao to his savings was to give him the required sum. Because he wasn't superstitious, because he didn't believe in luck or in any other occult force, after the incident with the controller, he had looked at his misfortune and had said to himself: "I am a good-for-nothing—I can't do anything . . ." This setback put his wedding far off into the future, when his mother would no longer be of this world, and he didn't even consider that the father could very well marry his daughter off to some richer prospect. In the midst of this drama, he'd met Odilia, whom he had liked immediately. Though it may appear unlikely, the idea of marrying her hadn't crossed his mind, even though he knew that the thought of her moved him: since the previous day, he had begun to doubt himself terribly. In fact, despite himself, he hadn't completely resigned himself to what had happened: to be honest, he hadn't stopped devising the plans that would allow him to get revenge against his destiny. If last night, in the bar, he had said to the young woman, "I would like to marry you . . . You are beautiful, I'm attracted to you; and I won't pay any money. I would like to marry you"—that would have represented a form of surrender, the recognition of his failure, the admission of his impotence. This was something he had always steadfastly refused to believe, despite Tonga, despite all the old men of Bamila. And finally, and this was far more serious, nothing said that the sick woman would have given her consent regarding Odilia.

He couldn't understand why he hadn't thought of it sooner. Odilia! The little sister about whom he had dreamed his whole life . . . He must have seen her several times before meeting her. How could he not have thought of it sooner? He might then have asked the young girl to extend her stay in the village. But, he reflected, on my own I would never have thought of asking her to marry me . . . Tonight he so badly wanted to touch her, to speak softly in her ear, to console her. And why was she not crying anymore? If only she could start crying again. Odilia! The loving little sister, devoted, and all that he had dreamed of . . . So his luck wasn't bad after all and no curse hung over him. Who could imagine a little sister as he had, who was tender and beautiful—whose very name was the same—and actually meet her in real life?

There is no way he could have thought of it by himself.

Yeah! Yet it was easy. It had taken all the concern of his mother, all her love for an ungrateful son . . .

He would go live in Fort-Nègre. He would work there. For Odilia, he would work twenty-four hours a day if that's what it took. For her, he would be careful to keep his arms tightly by his sides if a White man were to insult him: "Son of a bitch! Stupid nigger! Good-for-nothing savage! Monkey without a tail!" Or if a White man struck him. For her, he would be very careful not to strike a White man, careful no to get in trouble. Yeah! He would never forgive himself for abandoning Odilia, leaving her adrift among so many indifferent or even hostile men, in an immense city like Fort-Nègre! No, for that, he would never forgive himself.

For the first time, he felt less alone in this world whose strangeness, whose hostility, he could vaguely intuit, without exactly being able to grasp it. He had lost the disagreeable and humiliating feeling that he had been forced into a fight he was destined to lose. He still saw life as a cruel struggle without mercy, but now one could hope to win.

Odilia! His beloved little sister . . . And by the way, what did he actually know about the other girl? He had never had the opportunity to test her. Did she have Odilia's qualities, her poise? Even though he knew he would not have hesitated for an instant between the two, he nevertheless felt the need to compare, as if to better prove that he had gotten from life everything that he could possibly have hoped for.

He mopped his brow with the palm of his hand: with Banda, this was a sign of indecision. He turned to the young girl; their eyes met. Her mouth was set in an ironic expression: it looked as if she were egging him on. He said:

"So it's true?" He seemed to be pleading. "Is it true, you'd really do it?"

She simply nodded her assent. An ironic smile still floated across her lips and her dark eyes shone in the semi-darkness.

"You have a good soul," he concluded, without knowing that he was repeating the very same judgment his mother had made.

"I told you so," the sick woman chimed in, her face suddenly becoming animated. "I told you she was an angel sent from heaven. And know this: you won't have to pay a cent."

He approached her discreetly, very discreetly, until their shoulders were touching. He could feel her femininity radiating through her thin cotton dress, just as it had the previous night. She was just as warm, just as burning, just as quivering. For an instant the young man's sight clouded over, but he quickly got hold of himself. The contact with the fresh young body gave him a strange sensation that made him dream of tender and intoxicating things, as if the young girl were imposing her own universe.

He didn't even hear the purring of the car stopping in the street. After Odilia had given him a little shove, he rose stiffly, took the suitcase and went outside.

All that he would remember of the scene was that Demetropoulos had the voice of someone who had been castrated, that he was hysterically happy, that he counted out into his hand ten one thousand franc bills and that he tapped his shoulder. And also that his wife, under the violent light of the headlamps, had red and sickly lips, that she shook his hand and that her hand was cold and limp.

And finally, that he looked at the big black car with its prominent headlamps, remembered the controllers and the regional guards, smiled, and brought his hand to the black eye whose swelling had completely disappeared.

EPILOGUE

BANDA'S MOTHER DIED a few days after the events described here. Before leaving Bamila, Banda waited an appropriate amount of time.

On the day that had been set for his departure, he found himself surrounded by a number of people. Among them were, most notably, his uncle, the tailor from Tanga, his uncle Tonga from Bamila, Sabina, Regina, and the five women who had helped carry the cacao to Tanga, his poor mother's faithful friends . . . He had bid them farewell. He had told them that there was no longer any reason to continue living in Bamila now that his mother had departed.

"But Banda," Sabina had protested, "it was also your father's village! And what about the cacao plantation that he left you?"

"Who," the orphan responded, "ever said that the son absolutely had to live in the same place as the father? I'll go live in Fort-Nègre. Perhaps I'll return to Bamila after five, or twenty, or thirty years, who knows? Perhaps then everything will have changed: the old people will be dead and then we'll be able to breathe . . ."

The women were tearing up. The tailor remained sad and pensive.

"Son," he wound up saying, "if there is one man who would prevent you from going to the city, it's not me. I've always said that you would be better off in a big city; Fort-

Nègre is really what you need. I give you my blessing son—
be happy." And he had spit on the ground. It was an old-
fashioned way of giving your blessing.

"And to say that our children are only waiting for us to
die to leave like this . . ."

"If we leave," Banda had protested, though the useless-
ness of trying to explain left him drained, "it isn't always
with a joyful heart."

Tonga, for his part, had not said a word. He had limited
himself to looking fixedly at the ground, frowning, while
he stroked his chin in a perplexed manner.

Odilia's family had rapidly adopted Banda, and he
quickly became their favorite, their only son, now that Koumé was dead. And "his little sister" was his for life.

He wondered what he would have become if he had not
met Odilia. It seemed to him that they had to meet one day
or another, it seemed to him that it would have been impossible not to marry her. For the first time since his ado-
lescence, he took pleasure in life. He admired this tranquil
country whose inhabitants had inherited a unique sincerity
and harmony. But he also felt that this was just one step and
that soon he would have to be on his way again . . . Each day
he put off the deadline. His parents-in-law had shown little
enthusiasm at the prospect of his going off to the city, but
they hadn't opposed this project either.

And he, for his part, asked himself when he would go
to Fort-Nègre. Bamila had rejected him. Fort-Nègre, with
Tanga firmly planted in his memory, seemed hostile to him.
For the time being, he took refuge in Odilia's love, in the
strange ambiance of comfort and ease in which the little
sister bathed him. But he also felt he couldn't stay there.

One day he would have to try to conquer Fort-Nègre, he
couldn't stop halfway.

And the voice, his voice, whose inflections, its every in-
tonation, he liked to hear, kept whispering to him: "Banda,
what are you waiting for to leave? Aren't you ashamed? Get
up, take your wife, and leave . . ."

THE END

MONGO BETI (1932–2001) was born in Cameroon. He is considered one of the foremost African writers of the independence generation. His novels in English include *King Lazarus, Mission to Kala,* and *The Poor Christ of Bomba* (which was named one of Africa's 100 Best Books of the 20th Century).

PIM HIGGINSON is an Associate Professor of French and Francophone Studies at Bryn Mawr College. He is the author of *The Noir Atlantic: Chester Himes and the Birth of Francophone African Crime Fiction* (2011).

CPSIA information can be obtained at www.ICGtesting.com
Printed in the USA
LVOW061139190113

316380LV00001B/1/P